GHOST POST
LUKE TEMPLE

You can read the exciting first chapter of

DOORWAY TO DANGER

at the back of this book!

Luke Temple was born on Halloween, 1988. When he was 10, Luke didn't enjoy reading, he was terrible at spelling and he found writing hard work. Yet today he's an author! When not behind his desk with his writing partners, a one-eyed dog and a bald hamster, Luke spends most of his time visiting schools and bringing his stories to life with the children he meets.

Collect all the 'Ghost Island' series:

- ☑ Ghost Post
- ☐ Doorway To Danger
- ☐ The Ghost Lord Returns

Other books by Luke Temple:

- ☐ Stormy Cliff
- ☐ The Secret Theatre

To find out about Luke Temple and his books, including fascinating facts, fun videos, interviews and hidden secrets, visit:

www.luketemple.co.uk

Spooky Steve, ghost hunter and TV star, is one of the main characters in this book. Why not check out his website, full of photos, interviews, jokes and ghost-hunting tips:

www.spookysteve.co.uk

GHOST POST

LUKE TEMPLE

Gull Rock Publications

For Kieran

With thanks to Jessica Chiba, Anne Finnis, Gareth Collinson, Mike and Barbara Temple, Pete and Kath Murray, the children of Laburnum Grove Junior School and the children of Oxford Road Primary School

www.luketemple.co.uk

First published in Great Britain by Gull Rock Publications

The paper used in the printing of this book has been made from wood grown in managed, sustainable forests.

ISBN: 978-0-9572952-0-9

Printed and bound by CPI Group (UK) Ltd, Croydon, CR0 4YY

A catalogue record of this book is available from the British Library

Prologue

Pitch black.

The islanders of Holywell screamed.

Steve smiled to himself.

'And cut,' came the director's voice from behind the camera.

The lights around them flickered back on and they found themselves once again in the living room.

'Did you feel it?' said one islander.

'Something brushed past me, it was so creepy,' said a child.

'It was the ghost of Gertrude Spencer, as I had sensed!' said Steve dramatically.

'But how did you know?' whispered an elderly lady. 'How did you know that her g … ghost was here?'

'I used all my powers to bring her back to the room she died in, over two hundred years ago. That's why they call me Spooky Steve, ghost hunter!' He winked at the camera.

The islanders all gasped and clapped in appreciation.

'OK, well done, everyone. This has been a great

episode,' said the director. 'Steve, if you could do your final piece to camera, then we can all go for a coffee.'

Steve stared into the camera lens, his trademark spooky look on his face. 'So ends another episode of *Hunting Ghosts* with me, Spooky Steve. We came to this house on Holywell Island expecting to find the spirit of Gertrude Spencer, and in a dramatic ending she came to us in all her ghostly glory. Wasn't it an amazing way to end our ninth series? In the first episode of the next series we journey to Thistlewick Island, said to be one of the most haunted places in the world. Do join us then, if you can bear to watch!'

'And cut there,' said the director.

Thistlewick Island

Explore an interactive map of Thistlewick
at: **www.luketemple.co.uk/map.html**

Becky Evans was excited.

Very excited.

Mrs Didsbury, who ran the craft stall, had told her the news. She had overheard Mr Finch the carpenter talking about it.

Becky had to tell Jimmy. She ran across to his house at the edge of the market square and threw open the back gate. Her best friend was lying flat on the grass, aiming what looked like a miniature cannon at a dustbin – it was his latest experiment. A large ball of paper shot out of the cannon, soared through the air and landed in the dustbin.

'Come on!' she called to him.

'What?' Jimmy replied, turning the cannon around and aiming it at her. He loaded another ball of paper into it, pulled a piece of string, and the paper flew at Becky.

Without blinking, she caught it in her left hand, then walked over and pulled Jimmy upright.

'Becky, what are you …'

'You'll never guess who's coming to Thistlewick! There's a poster outside the island hall. Come on, let's go have a look!'

1

They charged out of the market square, down Water-splash Lane, and were at the island hall in no time. There was already a large group of people standing around the noticeboard in the entrance, talking animatedly.

Becky pushed her way to the front of the group, dragging Jimmy with her. They looked past the usual notices – 'Cake sale', 'Knitting club', 'Lost cat: have you seen Oakley?' – and stared up at a large poster. It read:

*'**Hunting Ghosts with Spooky Steve!** The world famous ghost hunter and his TV crew will be coming to Thistlewick Island on Monday 5th April. They've heard that your island has plenty of spooky tales to tell, and Steve will be sure to investigate them. So get those ghost stories ready, because soon you're going to be on TV!'*

Surrounding the writing on it were many cartoon ghosts, but the most prominent image was of a man's face, wearing thick-rimmed glasses and a strange look – Spooky Steve himself.

Becky stared at the poster for a long time, hardly believing what she was reading.

'The fifth of April – that's tomorrow!' She grinned at Jimmy and he smiled back.

Around them, other islanders were firing a barrage of questions at Mayor Merryweather, who had organised the whole thing. His teeth shone as brightly as the large chain around his neck as he spoke.

'How did you get the TV crew to come to Thistlewick, Mayor Merryweather?'

'It was a tough ask, I can tell you. They were very reluctant at first, but I persuaded them it was too good an opportunity to miss, what with all the ghosts we have here.'

'Where is Spooky Steve going to investigate first?'

'I can't say I know, yet, Mr Fishwick,' the mayor replied.

'Could he come to my house? I've a whole family of ghosts in my attic.'

'You'll have to ask the man himself when he arrives, Mrs Windybank.'

A round man with a twirly moustache, Mayor Merryweather was 70 years old, and the youngest mayor on Thistlewick for a long time. He had been largely responsible for the modernisation of the island, which was over an hour's boat ride from the mainland. Before his time in charge, there had only been one TV – at the White Wing pub and hotel – and no one had even heard of a computer. Now, Thistlewickians could regularly be found surfing the internet (or interweb as Mayor Merryweather called it), and most houses had televisions.

Inviting a TV crew to the island was Mayor Merryweather's latest bright idea, and seemed to be causing a great deal of excitement.

No one was more excited than Becky.

***

'In the first episode of the next series we journey to Thistlewick Island, said to be one of the most haunted places in the world. Do join us then, if you can bear to watch!'

Becky and Jimmy watched the end credits of *Hunting Ghosts with Spooky Steve* roll. It had been a brilliant episode – Spooky Steve lived up to his name, finding the ghost of Gertrude Spencer and lots of other ghostly goings-on on Holywell Island. Each time he made a new discovery, Steve said, 'Isn't it amazing?' Becky decided that she would use this phrase at every opportunity.

She flicked the TV off and turned to Jimmy. 'We're going to be on TV with Spooky Steve! Isn't it amazing?'

The two children were sitting at either end of Becky's living-room sofa, as they did each week to watch the latest episode of their favourite TV show. Becky's mum was the Thistlewick postmistress, and she and Becky lived together in the flat above the post office in the market square. Like most places on the island, the post office and flat were rambling and higgledy-piggledy, with oddly shaped rooms held up by wooden beams you could knock your head on if you didn't know when to duck. When they were younger, Becky and Jimmy had loved making up adventures around her home, pretending that the spiral staircase linking the flat to the post office actually led to a dangerous dungeon, and that Becky's bedroom door opened to reveal a gold-filled chamber.

'But why is Spooky Steve coming to film on

5

Thistlewick tomorrow?' asked Becky. 'The new series isn't on TV until June.'

'TV programmes are always filmed a long time before they're shown on TV,' Jimmy replied. He always seemed to know the answers to Becky's questions.

'Do you want to be on TV, Jimmy?'

'Not really,' he replied.

'You could have your own science show. *Jimmy Cole and the Big Bang*!'

'It would be too dangerous doing real science experiments,' said Jimmy. 'I've read about scientists getting blown up when they use the wrong chemicals.'

'Don't be so boring,' said Becky. 'It would be *amazing*!'

She longed to be a TV star like Spooky Steve. Jimmy was still happy to play games and make up pretend experiments in his garden; but Becky wanted a real adventure. If she was on TV, she would have them all the time! Now *Hunting Ghosts* was coming to Thistlewick, this was Becky's big chance.

'Do you think I'd be good on TV?' Becky asked.

'I think you would be *amazing* on TV,' said a voice from the doorway.

Becky turned to see her mum smiling at her – she had obviously been listening to their conversation from the kitchen.

'Oi, don't steal my catchphrase, Mum!'

'It's Spooky Steve's catchphrase, actually,' Jimmy pointed out.

Becky gave them both a mock glare.

'You shouldn't get too excited, love,' said Mum. 'The TV crew are going to be investigating the ghosts of Thistlewick, not a girl who wants to be famous.'

Becky rolled her eyes. Mum didn't get it. 'I don't just want to be famous. I want to be a TV star and have lots of exciting experiences, like Spooky Steve does.'

'Well, I'm not sure how much of an exciting experience Spooky Steve is going to have when he gets here. I can't say I really believe in all this ghost business.'

'Mum, you live on one of the most haunted islands in the world and you don't believe in ghosts?'

'I think they make very good stories and there are certainly lots of those about Thistlewick. There are also many good storytellers, especially the fishermen, and I think they enjoy making up these tales to frighten people. What about you two? Do you believe in ghosts?' Mum asked.

'I've read loads about them, so they could be real,' said Jimmy.

Becky frowned. She wasn't really sure if ghosts existed. Sometimes at school the classroom cupboard opened by itself. Becky's friends said it was the ghost of the old head teacher spying on them, but they were probably just making it up to scare each other. It had definitely worked on Jimmy – he never went near that cupboard! And last year, Becky had been sure she'd seen a boat floating out at sea in the middle of a storm, only for it to vanish into thin air – but that had probably been her imagination.

'I don't think I've seen one yet,' she settled on saying.

Perhaps when Spooky Steve came tomorrow, she would not only get to be on TV, but she'd also see her first ghost. Now that would be an amazing adventure!

'Can Jimmy and me help you deliver the post tomorrow morning, Mum?'

'Yes … of course you can, love.' Mum couldn't hide the surprise in her voice. 'If Jimmy wants to, of course?'

Jimmy considered it for a moment, then nodded.

'But you do realise what time you'll have to get up if you want to help, don't you?'

'Yes,' said Becky. 'Can we deliver the letters to the harbour?'

'Oh, I see,' said Mum. 'That's why you want to help. The TV crew are arriving at the harbour tomorrow morning, aren't they?'

'Yep. And it's going to be *amazing*!'

2

Spooky Steve

Becky's alarm went off at six a.m., but she was already awake.

She stared at the drawings of pirates, dragons and ghouls on the wall next to her bed and smiled. *Today I'll have a real adventure!*

Becky jumped out of bed. She chose her clothes far more carefully than normal. Sifting past the crumpled up T-shirts in her chest of drawers, she found a folded white one she hadn't worn for a while; out of her wardrobe she pulled her neatest pair of jeans. Becky's hazelnut hair usually flumped about like a fiddled-about-with mop, but she stuck a comb through it until it looked tidy enough.

Checking her reflection in the mirror on the wardrobe door, she saw her bright blue eyes shining back at her. Mum said they were the brightest she had ever known, and Becky wondered how they would look on camera.

'Becky Evans, ghost hunter!' she said in a dramatic voice, pointing at the mirror and winking. 'She's *amazing*!'

9

She jumped at the sound of Mum laughing from the hallway.

'I still can't believe you're up this early during the school holidays. Come on, love, Jimmy's waiting for us downstairs.'

They climbed down the spiral staircase from the flat to the post office and Mum headed into the sorting room behind the counter. Becky did a double take when she saw Jimmy standing by the stationery shelf.

'What are you wearing?' she asked, not sure whether to laugh or be shocked. Her small, dark-haired friend had on the brightest yellow shorts she had ever seen.

'Mum wanted me to dress smartly for the TV crew,' he replied.

'You'll blind them with those shorts if you're not careful!'

Mum walked over to them and handed Becky a large bag of post.

'I'll take my bike and do the delivery in north Thistlewick,' she said. 'You two can stay here in the south and deliver these by foot.'

***

Thistlewick was only six kilometres end to end, from the rough rocky beaches in the north, through the dark forest at the centre, to the gentle waters of the harbour in the south. But the hundred or so houses on south Thistlewick were very spread out, and the postal round felt like it was taking forever that morning as Becky and Jimmy trudged from place to place. Usually Mum delivered post to both north and south Thistlewick on her own – Becky didn't know how she had the energy!

When they finally reached the harbour, air was fizzing in Becky's lungs, and the light shimmering on the sea had a golden tint, which promised a glorious day.

Becky ran up to Albert Gailsborough, Thistlewick's oldest fishermen, and thrust the post into his hand. 'When are the TV crew getting here? Are they arriving on the Thistlewick ferry?'

'They're comin' in their own boat, so they won't be with us before the seagulls return from their mornin' catch,' Albert replied.

Guessing that meant a bit of a wait, Becky and Jimmy positioned themselves on top of a barrel of fish by the water's edge. The harbour around them was only small, with a few traditional boats and a rickety old hut. The fishy smell was strong but pleasant – you couldn't grow up on Thistlewick without becoming used to the smell of fish!

As the minutes ticked by, a small crowd gathered behind them. Mayor Merryweather arrived first, wearing his ceremonial royal-purple robes – it also looked like he'd given his golden chain a polish. There were lots of children, most of whom Becky knew and waved to. People from the market had turned up, taking a break from setting up their stalls, and Becky was surprised to see that even Mr Potts, one of Thistlewick's farmers, had come from the north of the island to see the spectacle. She felt secretly annoyed that so many people were there.

Albert looked up and, as if on cue, a colony of seagulls came diving over the harbour wall and landed on the fishermen's hut, looking as round and regal as the mayor.

'I can see a boat!' called a young child a few minutes later.

Sure enough, when she squinted out into the sparkling blue sea, Becky saw a dark object on the horizon. She felt a rush of excitement as she watched it moving towards her. By the time the big, shiny boat pulled up to the harbour wall she was quite nervous. It gave a roar as its jet engine turned off.

The first person to step out of the boat was a scruffy-looking man in blue baseball cap.

That's not Spooky Steve, she thought.

Mayor Merryweather walked over to him and Becky heard the man introduce himself as Craig, the director of *Hunting Ghosts*. Another man stepped onto the shore, carrying several huge boxes, which Becky guessed were full of camera equipment.

As the mayor greeted them loudly in turn, another

figure rose from the boat; Becky recognised him immediately. The Hawaiian shirt covered in flowers and the orange shorts that nearly matched Jimmy's in brightness may have made him look anything but spooky, but the thick-rimmed glasses gave it away – it was Spooky Steve. A gasp came from the islanders behind Becky as they all realised who he was too.

'Hello!' she said, jumping off the barrel and running over to him. 'My name's Becky Evans. It's *amazing* to meet you!'

He glanced down at her. 'Hello, Becky, nice to meet you too.' Then he saw Jimmy hovering by the barrels. 'Nice shorts – you have good taste.'

Jimmy gave him a small smile.

'If you need—' Becky began.

'Steve, we need to get started,' the director cut in, ignoring Becky and walking Steve away from her.

If you need anyone to help you, I can, she finished her sentence in her head, watching as the cameraman set up the biggest camera she had ever seen. It looked really complicated, with lots of different coloured buttons to press.

'Let's go for a take,' said the director a few minutes later. 'Action.'

The camera started recording and Steve said, 'So, we've just arrived on the beautiful island of Thistlewick; but don't let that beauty fool you – Thistlewick is said to be one of the most haunted locations on earth. There have been hundreds of ghosts reported here, which means it's the perfect place for me to come ghost hunting.'

As he spoke, Steve started walking along the harbour and the camera followed him. With a jump of delight Becky realised they were moving towards her. Were they about to interview her?

'Hang on, cut, cut, cut!' called the director. 'What's that girl doing in shot?' Becky froze as he stared at her. 'Would you move out of the way, please, little girl.'

She glared at him and walked over to join Jimmy, who was fidgeting nervously at the front of the crowd.

'Take it from there, Steve,' said the director. 'Action.'

'Thistlewick Island gets its name from the adventurer, Lord Samuel Lewis Thistlewick, who discovered the island while on an expedition, fell in love with it and came to live here in the eighteenth century,' Steve continued. 'And let's hope we come across Lord Thistlewick's ghost this week. Over the years there have been plenty of strange appearances from many other spectres and spirits across Thistlewick Island, which means this should be one of the most amazing episodes yet of *Hunting Ghosts* with me, Spooky Steve!'

He looked straight into the camera and pulled what Becky recognised as his 'spooky' face.

***

Becky spent the whole morning following the TV crew around as Steve interviewed some of the islanders. She was determined to get on camera by the end of the day, but plucking up the courage to ask for an interview was hard.

'Can you ask him for me?' she said to Jimmy as they watched the crew set up at the island hall to interview the mayor. 'Then you could be interviewed with me. After all, Steve said he liked your shorts.'

'I don't really want to,' said Jimmy, and soon after that he disappeared off home.

Mayor Merryweather spent most of his interview asking the cameraman about his camera equipment. When Steve eventually got him to discuss ghosts, the mayor said they should talk to Albert Gailsborough.

'He's the oldest person on Thistlewick, a fine fisherman and famous for his ghostly tales. You'll find him at the White Wing pub eating his lunch now. Why don't you join him? The landlady, Ms Galway, does a cracking fish surprise.'

As the crew walked down from the island hall and headed onto the coastal path, Becky shuffled along behind them building up her confidence. By the time they reached the White Wing pub at the south-western tip of Thistlewick, she was determined to ask for an interview.

As the grand building came into view, she ran up to Steve.

'Ah, Bethany, isn't it?' he said.

'It's Becky. Do … do you think you could interview me later?'

Steve puffed out his cheeks and called to the director, 'Craig, do you want to film this girl?'

The director gave her an unenthusiastic look. 'We're only talking to important people at the moment, little girl.'

Becky glared at him. She wanted to stick her tongue out, but stopped herself – if she was to stand any chance of getting on TV, she would have to be polite.

***

Albert stared suspiciously from the director's baseball cap to the camera in front of him, the deep wrinkles on his forehead furrowed in a frown, his straggly beard twitching.

'I s'pose you could interview me. Depends what it's about.'

'I would like to ask you about ghosts, Mr Gailsborough,' Steve said loudly.

'Oh, well there's many a story I could tell you about ghosts,' said Albert, perking up quickly. 'And call me Albert.'

Becky watched from a nearby table, sipping quietly on the strawberry boater drink she'd bought from the bar. Albert always jumped at every opportunity he had to tell a tale. She remembered one night when she was eight, she and her friends had sat around a campfire for a whole hour listening to Albert talk about his ghostly encounters out at sea. He had successfully managed to give her and Jimmy sleepless nights for a whole week!

'Roll camera. And action,' said the director.

'So, Albert …' Steve began.

'Excuse me,' came the cheery voice of Ms Galway. 'I've got your lunch, Albert. Extra tuna, just as you like it. And here's your drink, Steve.'

She grinned widely into the camera. Becky was sure Ms Galway had waited until exactly the moment the camera started filming before she went over to Albert's table. Some people would do anything to get on TV!

'Tell me about the ghosts on Thistlewick,' Steve began when Ms Galway had wandered off.

Albert leant forward and spoke in a low, dramatic voice. 'When I go out in my boat, I often come across the spirits of the poor souls who drowned off our shores. There's also them ghosts that are more of the scary variety. The kind that'll put a curse on you for comin' near their sunken ships. Even the seagulls fear goin' near 'em. I remember when I was ten, on my first trip out to sea—'

'Sorry, if I could stop you there, Albert,' Steve interrupted. 'We found quite a few shipwrecked ghosts last series. Could you tell me what you know about the ghost of Lord Thistlewick himself? After all these years, you must have seen him a few times.'

'There's no story to tell, I'm afraid,' said Albert, quite put out that he'd been interrupted. 'So far as I know, no one has ever seen the ghost of Lord Thistlewick.'

'Oh …' Steve looked rather disappointed. 'I know Lord Thistlewick had a daughter. Have you seen her ghost, at all?'

'I haven't. But I do know about the ghost of Little Lord Thistlewick!' Albert said eagerly. 'Lord Thistlewick's son. He died on his tenth birthday – fell off his horse down on Barefoot Bay. His ghost still haunts the caves round those parts.'

'Excellent. That sounds like the place we'll head to for our first ghost hunt.' Steve glanced at the director, who nodded in confirmation.

'We need to round up some people to come along tonight,' he said.

Becky shot up from her table, knocking her drink over. 'I can do that!'

The director sighed. 'OK, little girl, get a few people and bring them down to Barefoot Bay at nine o'clock for our first ghost hunt.'

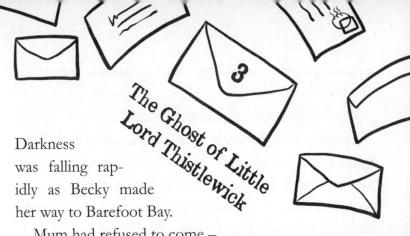

Darkness was falling rapidly as Becky made her way to Barefoot Bay.

Mum had refused to come – she still thought it was nonsense, and besides, she had to prepare the post to be shipped to the mainland the next morning. Becky had persuaded Jimmy to come after she promised he wouldn't be interviewed, and about twenty other islanders turned up too.

'Looking forward to your first ghost hunt with Specky Steve?' asked Finn, Albert's grandson. He was the same age as Becky and Jimmy, but far too annoying to be a friend.

'Don't make fun of him, Finn, or he won't want you to be in his TV show,' said Becky.

'I'm not bothered about being on TV. I'm coming along to see a ghost. I've seen them before, of course, but this should be a good one.'

'You haven't seen a ghost before,' Becky argued.

'Have. There've been loads when I've gone out in granddad's boat.'

'Liar.'

'Can you two stop?' said Jimmy. 'People are staring at us.'

By day, Barefoot Bay was a beautiful, golden stretch of sand with a stunning view out to sea. But the dark night made it seem eerie. As the unseen waves crashed against the black cliffs, the harsh sound was picked up by the wind and echoed strongly around the bay. It was the perfect setting for a ghost hunt, Becky thought.

'We're going to start filming in the centre of the bay,' said the director. 'Everyone, your job is to follow Steve and react to what he says.'

As they walked along the sand, Becky ran up to Spooky Steve. He had changed his clothes and was now wearing a dark shirt and trousers with a long, black leather jacket – his ghost-hunting gear.

'I did what you wanted, I got people to come along. Can I have an interview now?' she asked.

'We're about to start a ghost hunt, Betty, this isn't the time,' he snapped back at her.

'It's Becky,' she mumbled. Slightly hurt, she moved back to walk with Jimmy.

***

'I can sense something … someone.' Spooky Steve stopped dramatically and took a deep breath. 'There's someone nearby. I … I sense they're a very important person. Perhaps a Lord or a Lady. Is that right, Albert?'

'Yes, it's probably Little Lord Thistlewick, the son of Lord Thistlewick,' Albert said, fascinated.

'And … I'm getting an unhappy feeling. They're sad and angry. Does that fit?'

'It does,' Albert replied. 'Little Lord Thistlewick died here in seventeen-seventeen, fallin' off his horse.'

'Ah yes, I can sense him now. Perhaps he is sad about dying, or maybe he is annoyed that he fell off his horse. Whatever it is, something has kept his ghostly form here.'

Becky frowned. She didn't think Steve was sensing anything at all.

'He found all that out when he spoke to Albert at the pub,' she whispered to Jimmy.

'Hang on!' Steve exclaimed.

He froze and a glazed expression appeared in his eyes.

'Little Lord Thistlewick is trying to communicate with me. Yes. Hello, little man. He's trying to show me something. It's blocking out my vision. I need someone to guide me.'

'Ooh!' Becky raised her hand.

'Who's that waving at me?' Steve squinted. 'Yes, that boy!'

Becky turned slowly around and saw that he was pointing at Jimmy. Her friend looked as shocked as she was.

'I … I didn't wave. That was B-Becky,' he stuttered.

'Rubbish, go to Steve, boy, quickly,' said the director.

Jimmy edged forwards and let Steve grab his arm.

Becky frowned as Steve said, 'Jimmy, isn't it? I'll say where I need to go, your job is to guide me.'

It's the shorts, Becky thought. *Steve chose Jimmy because they have the same taste in stupid shorts!*

'Little Lord Thistlewick?' Steve called. 'Reveal your location to me.'

He waited. The camera, using night vision, panned from Steve and Jimmy to the reaction of the islanders. They were all silent, waiting for Steve's next move.

'That way.' He pointed to the cliffs. 'What's over there?'

'A … a cave,' said Jimmy.

Steve shot off quickly, veering from side to side as Jimmy guided him. Everyone followed.

They entered the tall cave. If outside had been dark, inside the cave was beyond black. Realising she could be helpful again, Becky felt her way to the front of the group.

'Do you want to use my torch?' she asked.

'No torches,' Steve replied sharply. 'The light might scare the ghost.'

'Move out of the way, girl,' the director hissed.

'Little Lord Thistlewick,' Steve said, his voice echoing strongly around. 'You have guided me to this cave, please make your presence known.'

Again they waited. Was there going to be a sound, a movement? Becky wasn't sure. She felt her heartbeat quicken. Were they about to see the ghost of Little Lord Thistlewick?

There was a gasp.

'What was that?' asked Steve.

'I ... I heard something,' whispered Albert.

They all listened carefully. Then there came a noise, over the sound of the sea – a loud scraping noise, like someone was scratching the walls of the cave.

'Was that you, little man? Give us another sign, to prove that you are with us.'

A large gust of wind blew through the cave. Becky felt her hair fly wildly around her. The air became very cold.

Her heart skipped a beat. She felt an icy chill run through her body. Something had grabbed her arm – a hand, a freezing cold hand! She let out a scream.

'Cut the cameras a moment,' said the director.

Steve turned around. 'What did you scream for?'

'Something's touching me!'

'Yes, something is touching you – it's that boy, you silly girl,' Steve said angrily, pointing to Finn. 'Your scream may just have scared our ghost off. I can't see him any more.'

Becky felt her face turn red with embarrassment. Finn was laughing quietly to himself beside her.

'Why did you do that?' she asked him.

'Scaredy cat,' Finn whispered so that no one else could hear.

Her heart was still beating fast, but before Becky had time to react, Steve exclaimed, 'No, there he is! Start the camera rolling – I hear hooves coming from outside! Jimmy, take me back to the cave entrance.'

Jimmy did as he was told. Becky strained her ears, but couldn't hear any hooves.

'They're getting louder.' Steve's voice was becoming more dramatic. 'I think Little Lord Thistlewick is reliving his fateful night for us. The horse sounds out of control, he's trying to calm it down. His voice is getting more panicked.'

I still can't hear anything, Becky thought. The people behind her pushed forwards, trying to see what Steve was looking at.

'They're … they're heading straight for me.' Steve's eyes were wide and fearful now. 'Little Lord Thistlewick is screaming. The horse, it's going to … Nooooo!'

Steve flew backwards, as if the horse had collided with him, and landed heavily on the ground.

'And there, the boy has fallen! I see him in front of me, at the edge of the cave. He's thin, with short black hair; wearing jodhpurs. Just curled up, in a lot of pain.' The camera focussed on the spot Steve was pointing at, where there was nothing Becky could see. Behind her,

Albert gasped. 'He's calling out. He's saying, "I'm sorry, I'm sorry." Maybe he's calling to his horse, that he's sorry he's hurt it.' Steve stood up and turned towards the camera. 'But we know now that Little Lord Thistlewick's ghost still haunts Barefoot Bay. And on that revelation, we'll bring to an end our first night here on Thistlewick. Hasn't it been amazing?'

'So how was the ghost hunt?' Mum asked the next morning over breakfast. 'You didn't say much last night.'

'It was OK,' Becky said, nibbling a rind of bacon.

'Did you see a ghost?'

'I'm not sure.'

It had taken her ages to get to sleep thinking about it. Had Spooky Steve really seen the ghost of Little Lord Thistlewick, or was he just making it up? The scratching on the cave walls had been pretty creepy, and the way the air had turned ice cold. But apart from that, she hadn't felt or seen anything strange. Maybe Mum was right, maybe it was all just stories made up to scare people.

Two bits of toast popped up from the toaster and Mum brought them to the table. 'I hear you got a bit frightened.'

'Who told you that?' Becky asked.

'Finn. I bumped into him on my rounds this morning. He said you screamed?'

For a second Becky thought she saw a grin forming on Mum's face. She glared at her.

'I'll make him scream later!'

'Becky, that isn't a nice thing to say.'

'Sorry … Mum?'

'Yes?'

'I need to find a ghost story I can tell Steve. Are there any about the post office?'

'We certainly don't have any ghosts, Becky. As for stories, there may be lots of ghost stories around Thistlewick, but as far as I know there aren't any involving this place.'

***

Becky climbed down the spiral staircase and walked through the post office into the market square. It was busy already, with islanders crowding around Albert, who was selling his fresh catch of fish, and the sound of Mr Finch sawing away at a tree trunk he was turning into a bench. Becky spotted an empty bench in between two red and white stripped stalls and moved towards it thoughtfully.

The only way she could think of getting an interview was if she had a really good ghost story to tell, but where could she find one that would impress Steve?

She felt a tap on her shoulder and turned to see who was there. No one.

She was about to sit down when there was a tap on her other shoulder. Still no one. Maybe it was her imagination.

'Boo!'

Becky jumped. Standing in front of her was a white sheet – or rather, someone wearing a sheet.

'Ooohhh! Did I scare you?' said the sheet. 'I am the ghost of Little Lord Thistlewick's horse. Neigh! Are you going to scream like you did last night? Are you going to run away?'

Stony-faced, Becky grabbed the sheet and tore it off.

'Shut up, Finn, you're not being clever.'

Finn stood there grinning like an idiot.

'I'll get you back for that,' Becky said hotly. 'And for telling my mum I screamed.'

'I'd like to see you try,' Finn retorted.

'Finn Gailsborough!' came a call from a nearby market stall. It was Mrs Didsbury. 'Give me my tablecloth back this instant – you're getting it dirty. I'll charge you for it if you're not careful!'

Now it was Becky's turn to grin. She watched Finn run off, then sat down on the bench to think. Maybe she could ask around the market for a ghost story, or get Albert to tell her one when he'd finished selling fish.

Becky noticed everything around her go quiet. Looking up, she saw the TV crew heading past. An idea formed in her mind, and as much as Finn was irritating, she had him and his white tablecloth to thank for it. She'd have to get Jimmy to help later, but her plan might just work.

'Excuse me!' she called.

The director turned around and glared at her.

'Please could I…'

'Not now, little girl!' the director nearly shouted at her. 'We're busy!'

Becky grimaced – she was getting annoyed with the director calling her 'little girl' all the time.

'But I know a really scary ghost,' she persisted. 'I promise it'll be one of the best ghosts you've ever heard about.'

The director continued walking, but Steve paused.

'If I interview you about this ghost, will you stop pestering us?' he asked.

'Yes!'

'Come on, Craig, let's interview Cathy.'

Steve walked over to her. He was wearing another horrible flowery shirt today with purple shorts and an odd-looking straw hat – it was like he'd got dressed in the dark.

'Last night at Barefoot Bay was pretty amazing, and this morning I encountered the ghost of Captain Penny at the graveyard. He usually only appears on his death day, but he came early just to see me. You need to give me something extra special to beat that,' Steve said.

'Make it good, little girl,' said the director, giving her a look that showed clearly he thought she couldn't tell them anything worth listening to.

He ordered the cameraman to get into position. The camera pointed straight at her, a microphone was positioned over her head, and they were ready to begin. Becky's big moment. She knew exactly what she was going to say.

'Action.'

'So, Cathy, before you tell me about your experience of ghosts, I'd like to ask you, as our youngest interviewee, what did you think of last night's ghost hunt?'

'It's Becky, and it was really scary when he was making all the noises, but then when you said he was sad about his horse, I felt sad for him too,' Becky fibbed.

'Excellent. So tell me about your ghost, Becky.'

'I haven't seen many ghosts,' she replied. 'But I think I've met one of the strangest on Thistlewick.'

Steve's eyes lit up. 'Where did you meet it?'

'In my home above the post office.'

'And what's so strange about this ghost?'

Becky thought fast. 'Well, we've worked out that his name's Joseph ... Joseph King. He used to live there and likes playing with the post, but he doesn't like it when people come to stay in our spare room. When we have guests round, during the night he throws letters from the post office at them and gives them paper cuts. I had to sleep in there once while my room was being painted, and I woke up with cuts all over my fingers.'

'OK, that certainly sounds like something we should investigate. Would your mum be happy for us to come round this evening to have a look for Joseph?'

'Oh yes, she'd be very happy,' said Becky, grinning widely.

***

'I've got a white sheet, a bell, a feather and invisible thread,' Becky said to Jimmy. They were standing in the spare room, next to Becky's bedroom. There wasn't much in the room, just a bed in the middle, bedside cabinet, wardrobe, a vacuum cleaner and Mum's old rocking chair – they would have to work hard to pull this off. 'Do you have your cannon thing?'

'Yes.' Jimmy pulled it out of a bag. 'Are you going to tell me what this is all about? Exactly what are we going to do with all these things?'

'We're going to give Spooky Steve and that director the scare of their lives. If everything goes to plan they might even think that we're actual ghosts!'

'I'm not sure that's a good idea,' said Jimmy.

'I thought you'd say that, now you're all friendly with Steve – now that you're his little assistant.'

'Becky, I'm not. I didn't want to help him last night. It was really scary.'

'Right, then, you can help me scare him back,' said Becky. 'Then I might forgive you.'

'But I thought you wanted to stay on Steve's good side?' asked Jimmy.

'I do, sort of. Steve and his crew aren't going to know it was us, because we'll be hidden. I'm fed up of them forgetting my name and calling me "little girl", so let's hope we scare them! If it all goes well and my ghost story makes it into the TV show, that's even better. They'll be here in twenty minutes, so we need to get everything set up.'

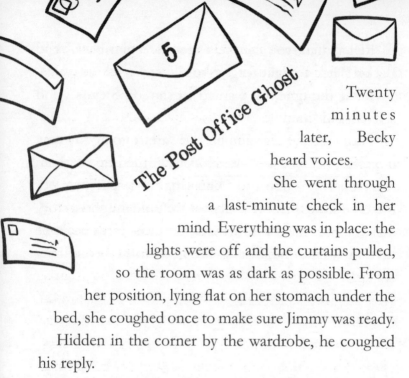

5

The Post Office Ghost

Twenty minutes later, Becky heard voices.

She went through a last-minute check in her mind. Everything was in place; the lights were off and the curtains pulled, so the room was as dark as possible. From her position, lying flat on her stomach under the bed, she coughed once to make sure Jimmy was ready.

Hidden in the corner by the wardrobe, he coughed his reply.

'Becky should be at home, I'm not sure where she's got to,' Becky heard Mum say from the stairway.

'Is it alright if we take a look around your spare room, though, Mrs Evans?' came Steve's voice.

'You do what you want. I don't know what she's been telling you, but feel free to go in and look. It's that door at the end. I'll be organising the post down in the sorting room if you need me.'

Becky heard the creak of several footsteps walking along the hallway towards the spare room. The door opened.

'Let's just have a quick look,' said the director. 'If that

34

girl's telling the truth and you can sense a presence, we'll do a proper investigation. If she's lying, there's no point in wasting our time.'

Becky watched through squinted eyes, and could just make out the cameraman and director entering the room. She grinned when she saw that the director was wearing gloves – to protect himself from paper cuts!

Steve followed them in. Just at the point he was in the doorway, Becky eased her grip on the piece of thread she had strung from her hiding place under the bed to the feather above the door. The feather floated downwards, just enough to brush against Steve's neck. As he turned around she quickly raised the feather up and out of sight. Steve frowned and turned back to face the room. Becky repeated her action, and this time the ghost hunter put his hand to his neck.

'Was that Joseph?' Steve called out to the room. 'Are you with us, Joseph? We're not going to do you any harm, but please show us that you're here.'

Becky put a hand over her mouth to stop herself laughing.

'Are you set up for night vision, Carl?' whispered the director.

'Yep. I'm ready to go,' the cameraman confirmed.

'OK, start filming, just in case.'

Becky heard a whirring sound and a beep as the camera began recording. It was time for her second action. She rang the bell gently. *Ding-a-ling-a-ling.*

'Blimey, it looks like Becky was right,' whispered Steve.

'That was a bell. You think a ghost would ring a bell?' the director said doubtfully.

'It's happened before. Can you give us another sign, Joseph, to prove your presence in this room?' asked Steve.

It was all going to plan – that was Jimmy's first cue. Becky tried to picture what was happening. Jimmy would be aiming his cannon, loaded with envelopes, straight at Steve.

Sure enough, Becky heard the whoosh of paper flying through the air.

'Are you getting this on camera, Carl?' Steve asked excitedly.

The cameraman nodded.

'See, it's like Becky said would happen. Joseph just threw post at me.'

The director grunted and eyed up the corner of the room where Jimmy was hiding. 'I think something a good deal more alive caused that.'

Steve ignored him. 'Joseph, before we leave you in peace, please could you show yourself to me... Where are you, Joseph?'

As Steve continued, Becky saw through a gap that the director was walking over to the bed. Surely he couldn't have seen her. She didn't dare move, but her eyes followed him as he started to bend down. Becky stifled a gasp as she realised what he had spotted – her foot had been sticking out. She quickly pulled it in, but it was too late.

'Becky told me that you don't like people coming into this room. Could you tell me why that is?' Steve was saying.

The director's arm reached under the bed, just missing Becky's leg. She was seconds away from being grabbed. What could she do?

She coughed twice and hoped Jimmy would hear and understand. In her original plan, the grand finale had involved Jimmy throwing a sheet in the air, as if an invisible ghost had sent it flying out of the wardrobe. But now Becky just wanted it to distract the director.

She heard Jimmy open the wardrobe door and watched as the sheet flew across the room, unfolded mid-air and floated down on top of the men. She peaked out from under the bed to see them desperately trying to untangle themselves. After her moment of panic it was a brilliant sight.

As they managed to pull the sheet off, there was a sudden scream. A loud thud followed, right above Becky's head – something had landed on the bed!

'I knew it,' the director exclaimed. 'I knew this was a set-up. What did you think you were playing at, boy?'

'Oh, it's Jimmy, the boy with the shorts,' said Steve. 'I suppose you're here somewhere as well, aren't you, Becky? You must have put him up to this.'

'She's under the bed!' the director said fiercely.

There was nothing she could do now. Her heart in her mouth, Becky slid out from under the bed. Lying on top of it in front of her was Jimmy. His eyes scanned the room madly and he looked terrified.

'Why did you go and give us away like that?' she whispered to him angrily.

'I … I don't know what happened,' Jimmy stuttered. 'One minute I felt something grab me, the next I was lifted up and thrown onto the bed!'

Becky stared at her friend, confused – that hadn't been part of the plan. It wasn't like Jimmy to get carried away.

'You can stop playing games with us, children.' Steve stared down at them. 'There isn't actually a ghost here, is there? You just made it all up. That was a stupid thing to do.'

Becky lowered her head and bit her lip.

'You can stop filming, Carl. They're not worth our time. Come on, Steve, let's get out of here,' said the director.

Steve nodded and walked over to the door. He tried to open it, but it didn't move.

'So you've locked us in as well. Let us out, right now!'

he shouted at Becky.

'I ... I didn't lock the door,' said Becky.

'What?'

'I didn't lock it.'

'Don't be so stu ... so stu ... so—'

Becky turned to see what had stopped Steve in his tracks.

She might have expected there to be a flash of light – a bang – an explosion – something to prepare her for what she saw now. But there was nothing. One moment it was a blank space, then in the blink of an eye there appeared the most horrifying thing she had ever seen.

The head that was floating in front of the door, almost nose to nose with Steve, was ancient and pale.

Becky froze stiff. The room around her was silent. They were all too scared to scream.

The mouth in the head slowly ached open. The eyelids flickered and opened to reveal lifeless eyes, like two holes leading to an empty soul.

The next thing Becky saw was Steve choking. Her eyes widened as a cracked, bony hand reached through the door and tightened around Steve's neck.

'Get off him,' yelled the director. He grabbed hold of the nearest thing to him – the vacuum cleaner – and tried to hit the hand with it.

The vacuum cleaner passed straight through the hand and knocked Steve square on the jaw. He fell backwards.

The head by the door opened its mouth wider, and a loud blowing sound started. Becky looked over to the director. The sound was coming from the vacuum cleaner – it had turned on. It wasn't even plugged in! The director staggered backwards, an invisible force making the vacuum cleaner attack him. He collapsed into a corner.

When Becky turned back to the door, there wasn't just a head and a hand – a leg appeared, then another, passing straight through the door, until the figure of a tall man soared into the centre of the room.

Becky felt very strange. The man looked so real, from his greased-back hair to his old-fashioned jacket and ragged shirt. But at the same time, it felt like he was only half there – like a shadow or a reflection. Not a complete person. A ghost.

'Are … are you the ghost of Joseph King?' asked Steve.

'No!' the ghost wheezed. It was barely a whisper – a choked voice that hadn't been used for a very long time. But at the same time the word filled Becky's mind powerfully.

'You'd better be getting this, Carl!' the director whispered hoarsely.

Carl, until now pressed rigid against the wardrobe, moved a trembling finger up to his camera and pressed record. The ghost moved a chilling hand towards the lens and it cracked. The camera was useless, and Carl collapsed to the floor.

Becky heard Jimmy gasp. She turned to face him, and the ghost had moved – he was there, standing over her friend, staring down. Jimmy shook wildly; she'd never seen him so scared.

'Stop it!' she shouted.

The ghost inclined his head towards her.

'Stop it!' Becky shouted again. She grabbed hold of Jimmy and pulled him off the bed. He stood beside her, still shaking.

The man started to move towards them. Not walking, but gliding along.

'Who … who are you?' Becky asked.

He edged closer.

Becky forced her eyes away from the ghost and down to Steve. 'Steve, help! Do something!'

'I can't,' Steve muttered from the floor, more terrified than any of them.

'You have to. You're the ghost hunter. You're the only one who can stop him.'

Steve closed his eyes and started breathing deeply.

Becky looked back to the ghost, but he had gone.

Before she had time to be relieved, though, an icy sensation ran through her. He was behind her, she knew it.

Turning slowly around, she saw the ghostly figure

leaning over her left shoulder. Becky stared straight at his face, barely centimetres from her own. It was twisted, contorted with rage, paler than any human's could be, almost glowing.

'I curse this post office,' the man whispered. 'Soon my curse will fall.'

He gave a small, cracked cackle and soared towards the floor, where Steve lay. The ghost shot straight through him and disappeared.

There were a few seconds' silence, then Steve let out a bone-chilling scream.

The door to the spare room flew open. Becky's mum was standing there.

'What on earth is going on?' she asked.

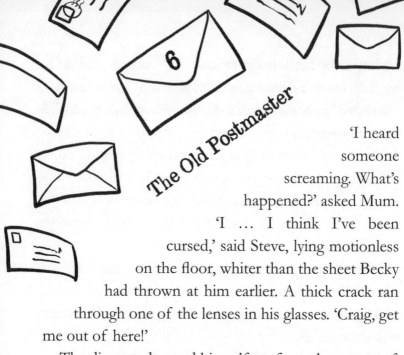

6

The Old Postmaster

'I heard someone screaming. What's happened?' asked Mum.

'I … I think I've been cursed,' said Steve, lying motionless on the floor, whiter than the sheet Becky had thrown at him earlier. A thick crack ran through one of the lenses in his glasses. 'Craig, get me out of here!'

The director dragged himself up from the corner of the room, scrabbled around on the floor for his baseball cap and pulled Steve up. They hurried out of the room, pushing past the others as they went. Still shaking, Carl the cameraman gathered together his camera equipment and followed them out.

'S-sorry,' he said to Becky as he went.

'Explain,' Mum said, staring at Becky.

'There was a ghost. He just appeared. It was really scary…' Becky began.

'For goodness' sake!' Mum exclaimed. 'What has Steve whoever-he-is got you believing in now? And you too, Jimmy? You look terrified.'

'It was real, Mum, I promise,' said Becky.

Jimmy nodded in agreement.

'You know, I thought that letting you search for ghosts was just a bit of harmless fun, but look at you both. Fun doesn't come into it – I will be complaining to Mayor Merryweather first thing tomorrow about Spooky Steve. I'm sorry I let him in the house! Now, let's calm you two down and get you something hot to drink.'

***

Becky sat up on the pillow at the end of her bed, tucked under the slanted ceiling of her bedroom. She looked at her drawings of the ghouls on the wall.

You're nothing like the real thing.

But Becky certainly wouldn't want the face she had seen earlier to peer down at her every time she went to bed. In fact, she never wanted to see it again.

In her mind she heard the creepy voice: 'I curse this post office. Soon my curse will fall.'

She'd tried her best to explain to Mum what had happened – not mentioning the bit about Jimmy and her pulling the prank, of course – but Mum was having none of it. Becky expected her to be angry, but she seemed more concerned, and had sent Jimmy home and Becky off to bed.

Becky expected to have lots of bad dreams, her mind repeating her experience in the spare room. But she slept quite well, and there was only one dream she could remember having. Not really a dream, just an image of a beautiful woman. Waves of dark hair blew around the woman's face; she had a smile full of life and eyes of sky.

When Becky woke, though, her mind was full of questions. Why had a ghost turned up and cursed the post office? Why had it chosen to do it last night? What would the curse do?

The post office didn't seem any different when she went down and checked – everything was in place, the bags of post all ready for Mum to deliver. She thought about what Jimmy would say. Becky would ask him about it later, but knew he'd probably suggest starting with the basics – she should figure out who this ghost was.

He'll probably have something to do with the post office.

As she had that thought, Becky noticed the small wooden plaque just inside the post office entrance. It was one of those boring things that had been there as long as she could remember, and which she had probably walked past thousands of times without paying the least bit of attention to.

On the plaque were the names of all the people who had run the Thistlewick post office since Lord Thistlewick set it up in 1712.

Could the ghost be one of the old postmasters, or someone connected to them?

She studied the sign carefully:

The Postmasters and -mistresses of Thistlewick Island
1712-1717: Walter Anion
1717-1761: Samuel Kimble
1761-1800: Benjamin Kimble
1800-1805: Isaac Dalton
1805-1855: Enoch Inverkip
1855-1880: Edwin Acklington
1880-1940: Herbert Acklington
1940-1988: Clement Shufflebottom
1988-1999: Braden Inverkip
1999-   : Barbara Evans

The only person she could rule out was Mum, who was, of course, alive, but also the only woman. The ghost was definitely a man.

Could she figure out from which period of history the ghost had come? She tried to visualise his clothing. It had been fairly simple, but seemed old fashioned – over a hundred years old, perhaps. That still only ruled out a few of the names.

As Becky stood there, she saw Mum through the window, walking across the market towards the post office, looking red faced and flustered.

'I've been to see the mayor,' Mum said when she opened the door. 'He says there's nothing he can do.

Spooky Steve has been taken ill and is bedridden at the White Wing. No one can disturb him. The TV crew aren't talking to anyone and will be leaving for the mainland if Steve doesn't get better soon.'

'Maybe Steve has been cursed – he said he had been last night. Maybe we're all cursed too, because we were there when the ghost came.'

'What are you talking about? There's nothing wrong with Steve. There is no ghost, and no curse, so put those thoughts out of your mind. Now, I'm late delivering the post and I've got to open up the shop. Can you deliver it for me, Becky?'

***

Becky couldn't concentrate on the postal round.

Steve had been taken ill, the TV crew would be leaving soon, and now Jimmy refused to come out of his room to see her.

'He hasn't had much sleep,' his mum had said when Becky had knocked on their front door to see if he'd come with her. 'He didn't say what happened last night, but it's given him a big shock. I have a good mind to complain about Spooky Steve, putting ideas in my son's head.'

'My mum already has,' said Becky.

Poor Jimmy, she thought as she cycled slowly through the forest to north Thistlewick.

She had forced him into helping her play a trick on Steve. She wouldn't be surprised if he never forgave her for it, let alone stepped inside her home again.

When Becky arrived at Half Acre Farm, she parked her bike in front of the farmhouse and knocked on the door. She didn't notice Mr Potts coming out to greet her.

'Becky? Becky?'

'Sorry, Mr Potts,' she said.

'You knocked on the door.'

'Oh, yes. I have this for you.' She handed him a thick-looking parcel.

'Excellent. Just in time,' said Mr Potts. 'My cows have been ill, you see, and this is the medicine I need to make them all better.'

The questions started firing through Becky's mind once more as she continued on her round. She stood staring at Mrs Turner's letter box, as if it would provide her with all the answers, when she realised she'd just put a letter meant for Mr Finch through it. She had to knock on the door and ask Mrs Turner for the letter back, so she could post it to Mr Finch next door. Then she managed to get a parcel for the musician, Mr Starr, stuck halfway through his letter box. It wouldn't budge. Becky knocked on his door but there was no reply and she remembered he was playing in a concert on the mainland. She just had to leave the parcel stuck where it was.

Fortunately, it was quite a short delivery – only thirty

pieces of post in all. By the time she got to the harbour, Becky wanted to talk to Albert about the ghost. He had, after all, seen more spooky things on Thistlewick than anyone else.

But the fisherman's boat wasn't moored up, which meant he was already out at sea. Finn was milling about, but she wasn't going to talk to him and just handed over the envelope addressed to his granddad. Her worries would just have to wait.

***

'You've spent all day wandering round the flat like a lost sheep,' Mum said later that afternoon.

'Have I? Sorry, Mum.'

Becky had actually been searching for clues about the post office ghost. She'd found nothing. No documents, or books, or anything like that.

'Right, I'll give you something to keep you occupied,' said Mum. 'There's a bag of old clothes by the stairs. I've been meaning to put them in the loft for a while. Why don't you take them up there.'

'The loft!' Becky exclaimed.

'Yes, the loft,' Mum replied suspiciously.

'Thanks, Mum.'

Becky ran off and found the bag of clothes. She may have searched the flat top to bottom, but Becky hadn't thought about the loft. Maybe she would find a clue there.

She pulled the ladder down from the loft and climbed up, poking her head through the small hole in the ceiling. She was greeted by a musty smell. Shining a torch around, Becky saw such a variety of items that she could search for days before finding anything even remotely helpful.

Fortunately, Mum had divided the space into two. To Becky's left were all their personal things and to the right were the post office archives. It was the items on the left that Becky knew well: in one box, there were bibs and rattles from when Becky was a baby, along with an envelope containing the hair from her first haircut; in another were all her old soft toys. She threw the bag of old clothes on top of some family photo albums and decided that she should focus on looking at the post office archives to the right of the loft.

She flicked through some dull books of numbers that didn't make sense to her. In a box of old papers she found information about Herbert Acklington, the postmaster from 1880 to 1940. Her eyes lit up. She read a short article from a 1940s newspaper about him being sadly missed now he had retired and moved to Australia, where he planned to spend his remaining years.

So he couldn't be the ghost.

She continued searching for what felt like hours. Box after box, book after book, not getting anywhere.

'Becky, what are you doing up there?' Mum called. 'You're taking forever.'

Becky stood up in the centre of the loft, careful not to bang her head on the slanted roof.

'I'll be down in a minute,' she said.

She shone the torch around, looking for any last clues. At the far end of the loft the torchlight shone over a painting of a man. Something about it looked familiar.

She moved closer. The writing at the bottom read: *Mr Walter Anion, Thistlewick Postmaster, 1712-1717.*

'I was given that painting a few years ago,' came Mum's voice. Becky turned around and saw her standing in the loft entrance. 'There's always been a mystery about the first postmaster on Thistlewick – for a long time nobody knew who it was. Then when they were clearing out the old Thistlewick prison, they found that painting and gave it to me. It was hidden under some floorboards there, for some reason. So now we know that the first postmaster was Walter Anion. I had his name added on the plaque in the post office and was going to hang the painting up, but it gives me the creeps. Anyway, love, tea's on the table. Hurry up.'

'I'm just coming,' Becky said quietly.

She turned to study the painting again. Looking at it sent a shiver down her spine. Staring back at her through the ornate frame was the pale, thin face of a man with greased-back hair and furrowed eyebrows. His green eyes may have been more human than they were in ghostly form, but they contained the same angry feeling.

I've found the post office ghost, Becky thought. *His name is Walter Anion!*

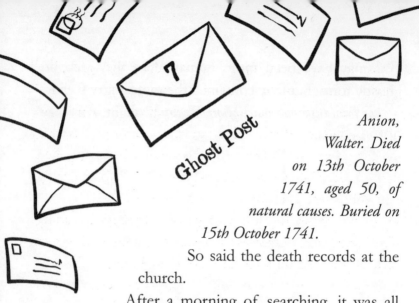

Anion, Walter. Died on 13th October 1741, aged 50, of natural causes. Buried on 15th October 1741.

So said the death records at the church.

After a morning of searching, it was all Becky had managed to find out about the old Thistlewick postmaster.

She had looked everywhere at home and had started browsing through books at the library, but none of them mentioned him. Mrs Turner, the librarian, suggested she should search the newspapers that were kept in the library attic, but they didn't go back beyond 1850, so were no good either.

If only she could figure out what made the ghost angry enough to curse the post office. Walter Anion had died in the eighteenth century, so his ghost had had about two hundred and seventy years to do it. Why had he appeared now?

Becky wished that Jimmy was with her. He loved reading and was brilliant doing research projects in school. If anyone could find something out about the ghost, it was Jimmy. Without him, Becky was stuck, but he still refused to come out of his room.

At least nothing else bad had happened. Steve was still ill in bed at the White Wing, and rumours were starting to spread across Thistlewick about what had happened to him, but Walter Anion's curse didn't seem to be having any other effects around the post office.

Becky sat in the library trying to focus on reading *Lord Thistlewick's Legacy* – there was so much writing that it took her ten minutes to read a single page. She was three minutes into page eight, when Mrs Turner walked up to her.

'I'm afraid I have to close the library for a while, Becky.'

'Oh, why's that, Mrs Turner?'

'Mayor Merryweather has called an emergency island meeting. You can come back to read your book in a couple of hours.'

'An emergency island meeting? What's it about?' Becky asked.

'I'm not sure,' Mrs Turner replied.

Curious, Becky followed the librarian to the island hall and joined the queue of people filtering inside.

She found Mum and squeezed into the seat beside her. She'd never known there to be so many people in the hall – all the seats were full and there were even people standing at the back. Jimmy and his mum were nowhere to be seen, though.

At the front, a small line of islanders sat next to Mayor Merryweather on the stage, all looking very concerned. The mayor himself was wearing an unusually sombre grey jacket.

'Hello all, thank you for coming along at such short notice,' the mayor began in a voice that matched his jacket. 'It has come to my attention today that some troubling situations have presented themselves, involving a number of islanders. On their own these situations could be considered simple bad luck, but together they are suspicious. These people you see beside me are just some of those who have been affected. I will ask them to explain what has been happening.'

'My cows are very ill,' said Mr Potts. 'I ordered medicine, but the wrong stuff was sent through. I gave it to them without realising and now they're even worse – they're not producing milk.'

Becky saw a tear run down the farmer's cheek and felt very uneasy – she had delivered that medicine to him.

Finn spoke up next. 'We haven't caught any fish since yesterday morning, have we, Granddad? Not a single one.'

Albert shook his head miserably. 'I've been out five times and not landed a single fish. It's not happened before, not ever.'

'I can't cut wood properly,' said Mr Finch angrily. 'Every time I go to carve something, it either snaps or goes wonky. Doesn't matter which saw I'm using. How's a carpenter supposed to work when he can't cut wood straight?'

Becky felt her heartbeat quicken as five more islanders listed their problems, and then a number of others raised their hands to say bad things had happened to them too.

'It is very difficult to connect any of these issues together,' said Mayor Merryweather. 'We only know that they all started happening yesterday, at the same time, incidentally, that we found out Spooky Steve was ill and his TV crew stopped filming for *Hunting Ghosts*. I have called you here now to ask if anyone has any idea what might be going on?'

Becky had a horrible feeling that she knew exactly what was causing the problems.

'Those were all people who I delivered post to yesterday,' she whispered to Mum. 'It's Walter Anion, he's cursed all the post.'

'Don't be silly, love,' said Mum, glancing uneasily around to check that no one had heard Becky.

'It's his curse, I know it is,' Becky persisted.

Mum stared at her. 'Be quiet.'

But Becky didn't listen. She raised her hand.

'Becky Evans, unless you want to get into serious trouble, put your hand down, now,' Mum hissed through gritted teeth. She looked around, embarrassed.

Becky reluctantly did as she was told.

'Very well,' said the mayor, when no one else spoke. 'We all need to keep a careful watch on what happens across Thistlewick in the next few days. A very careful watch indeed.'

***

A night of worry lay ahead for Becky. She didn't know what to do. Was it all nonsense, like Mum said – just Becky's imagination working overtime – or was the curse having an effect? It seemed too much of a coincidence that the day after the post office had been cursed, everyone who'd received post had suffered major problems – twenty-nine islanders in all!

The house was so quiet as she lay under her duvet – even the sound of the sea was softer than usual. It brought to Becky's mind her dad's favourite phrase, or what Mum said his favourite phrase had been, anyway: 'It's so quiet you can hear the dead think.'

Becky had never known her dad. Mum didn't talk about him much, but she'd told Becky that he had been a great adventurer, exploring the world. One day, just before Becky was born, he had mysteriously disappeared and never returned. Although she hadn't said it, Becky knew that Mum thought he was dead.

If there was one ghost I'd want to see, it would be Dad's.

Becky definitely did not want to meet the post office

ghost for a second time.

She just hoped that tonight she would see the image of the beautiful woman again. It had appeared in her dreams several times each night since she had first seen it.

She drifted off to sleep at about ten o'clock … only to be woken again a short while later.

At first Becky didn't open her eyes. She listened to the sound that had stirred her from her sleep. Something bumping gently on the floor, in a rhythmic sort of way.

Bump bump. Pause. *Bump bump.* Pause. *Bump bump. Bump bump.*

She opened her eyes and looked around. The noise was coming from somewhere outside her room. Curiosity led her to get out of bed and walk out into the hallway.

Bump bump.

It was coming from the spare room.

She crept over to the door, took a deep breath and opened it slowly. Highlighted in the moonlight, the rocking chair stood in the opposite corner, rocking slowly back and forth. But there was no one in it!

Bump bump. Bump bump.

She closed her eyes.

When she opened them again, the chair was rocking furiously.

Bump bump! Bump bump! Bump bump!

There was someone sitting in it now. Even through her fear, Becky saw it was Walter Anion.

He stared straight at her, even more terrifying as he glowed in the silvery moonlight.

'The curse will get worse!' he said to the rhythm of the rocking.

Bump bump. Bump bump.

Becky tried to move. She wanted to run back to her room, dive under her duvet and hide from him. But she was frozen, unable to do a thing.

'The curse will get worse, the curse will get worse, the curse will get worse tomorrow!' the ghost sang with child-like joy. It was like the creepiest nursery rhyme Becky had ever heard.

A strong gust of wind blew through the window. The ghost vanished.

Becky's fear remained. She stared at the rocking chair until she could stare no harder, as the rocking got slower and slower.

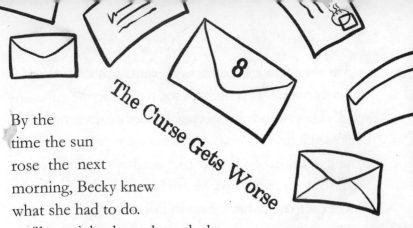

By the time the sun rose the next morning, Becky knew what she had to do.

She might have hoped the worst was over, that all the problems around Thistlewick would soon get better, but her second visit from Walter Anion told her for certain that his curse was only just beginning.

She would go to see the mayor and tell him all about it.

Throwing on her clothes and not bothering to comb her hair, Becky walked out into the hallway.

As she walked past the kitchen she stopped in her tracks.

Mum was sitting there, eating a slice of buttered toast and sipping orange juice. Nothing out of the ordinary about that. But in the toast rack, Becky saw a brown object – a letter.

'Who's that letter for?' she asked.

'Me, love,' Mum replied.

'Don't open it. Throw it away! Whatever you do, don't open it!'

'Becky, I'm getting quite fed up with your nonsense

now. It's my letter, I'll do what I want with it.'

Becky ran towards Mum as she picked up the envelope and slid her thumb between the folds to rip it open. As Becky leapt towards the table, a huge gust of wind swept around the kitchen – and the windows weren't open. Mum took a sheet of paper out and unfolded it.

'Give it to me, Mum,' Becky said, tugging on the letter.

'Hang on.' Mum pulled it away from her. A frown spread across her face. 'No, that can't be right.'

'What can't?'

'Look.' Mum laid the letter on the table for Becky to read.

At the top she recognised the official logo of the postal service. She began to read the writing underneath:

Dear Mrs Evans,

You will have read recently of the cutbacks that the postal service is having to make throughout the mainland and its associated islands. This includes Thistlewick Island.

We have weighed up our priorities very carefully, and I am saddened to tell you that an option we are strongly considering is the closure of the Thistlewick post office. If this is to go ahead, it will take effect one month from the date of this letter. Thistlewick's postal service will then be operated entirely from the mainland.

You will, of course, have a chance to consult with us about our decision. A series of meetings is being held for all those concerned, starting with one on the afternoon of Friday 9th April.

Yours sincerely,

John Charlton

John Charlton

Head of the Mainland Postal Service

'Mum ...' Becky's voice trailed off. She didn't know what to say.

Mum had her head in her hands. 'I don't understand it. I'd read about the cutbacks, but I never thought ... Why is this happening to me?'

Becky had a strong idea why it was happening. She didn't know how, but she was sure it was linked to Walter Anion in some way. Before she could explain, Mum shot up from the table.

'What's the date?' she asked.

Becky looked over to the calendar on the wall. 'The ninth of April.'

'Then that first meeting is happening this afternoon,' Mum said with horror. 'I ... I have to go. I have to save our post office!'

Everything after that happened in a whirlwind. Becky watched helplessly as Mum stuffed clothes and wash things into a bag and made a couple of phone calls. She went down to the post office and collected some official-looking documents, and an hour later she was ready to leave.

'If I go now I should just make the early ferry across to the mainland.' Mum looked at Becky. 'You're going to have to stay with Jimmy. I've rung his mum and she'll be over to fetch you in a minute.'

'But Mum…' Becky pleaded.

'Sorry, love, I have to go. I just have to.'

Mum gave Becky a quick hug and a kiss on the forehead, and then she was gone.

Becky stood speechless. In her mind, she heard Walter Anion's voice:

'The curse will get worse!'

***

'I should have stopped her from opening it,' Becky said, trying to hold back tears.

'You couldn't have done anything,' said Jimmy's mum. 'It wouldn't have changed the postal service's decision if your mum hadn't opened it, would it?'

'Mrs Cole is right, Becky. I cannot see how you could have stopped it,' said Mayor Merryweather.

Jimmy and his mum had arrived shortly after Becky's mum had left. On Becky's request, Jimmy had run to fetch the mayor and now the four of them were sitting round Becky's kitchen table, drinking cups of tea and staring at the letter.

'But don't you see?' said Becky. 'It's Walter Anion's curse. Everyone who received a cursed letter has had bad luck, which is stopping them from doing their jobs – Mr Finch can't cut wood straight, Albert can't fish. Even if Mum was always going to receive the letter, now she is cursed too, so she won't stand a chance of saving the post office.'

She looked sadly to Jimmy. He nodded slowly, understanding what had been going on.

'Who is Walter Anion, and what do you mean about the letters being cursed?' Jimmy's mum asked.

'I was going to come and see you this morning,' Becky told Mayor Merryweather. 'Before I found Mum with the letter …'

Slowly, she and Jimmy went through everything that had happened in the last few days. Becky explained her theory about Walter cursing the post office, and that meant all the post she had delivered too.

'I think that's why so many people have had things going wrong.'

'I see,' said the mayor, nodding thoughtfully.

'I'm sorry I didn't say anything before,' said Becky. Jimmy's mum put a soft arm around her. It wasn't like a hug from her own mum, but if felt comforting all the same.

'Well I'm glad you've told me now,' said Mayor Merryweather.

'Do you believe us?' she asked doubtfully.

'Yes, I think I have to, Becky, with everything that's happened. You have both been very brave.'

'I wasn't,' said Jimmy. 'After that night with the ghost I ran away. I never wanted to come in this place again. I'm sorry, Becky.'

'It's OK, Jimmy. I don't blame you. If you don't want to come here any more I understand. I'm scared too.'

'No, I'm going to help you,' Jimmy replied, his round face unusually determined. 'You'd be useless without me, anyway.'

Mayor Merryweather stood up. 'I must call another island meeting. It's time to explain to everyone what we think has been happening.'

***

The nervous chatter that filled the island hall stopped abruptly as Mayor Merryweather spoke up from the front. He explained everything that Becky and Jimmy had told him. As he talked about the curse and the post office, people slowly started to turn around to stare at Becky, who was sitting at the back of the hall. She sunk down in her chair.

'Achoo!'

The sneeze was so loud it stopped the mayor mid-sentence. Everyone turned away from Becky to see where it had come from.

'Are you alright, Mr Starr?' asked Mayor Merryweather.

The people around the musician started to gasp and edged away from him. Becky strained to see what had happened. Her eyes widened as she saw what Mr Starr was holding up. A parcel. The parcel that she had tried to deliver and that had got stuck in his letter box. Becky put her head in her hands – she had completely forgotten that Mr Starr hadn't been on Thistlewick when she'd delivered the post. She should have removed the parcel from his letter box before he had returned.

'I got back home ten *achoo* … ten minutes ago. Found the parcel in my *achoo* … letter box. Right then I started *achoo* … sneezing. Then this meeting was called and I came *achoo* … here. Does this mean I've been cursed?'

'I'm afraid I think it does, Mr Starr, I am sorry,' said the mayor, but he was barely heard. Now everyone was talking frantically.

People around Becky were asking each other if they had received a letter, whether they had been cursed. A few glared at her again.

The noise was only broken when Mr Finch called out, 'What do you intend to do, Mayor Merryweather? How are you going to stop this curse?'

'Well, the post office has been temporarily closed. Unfortunately, Barbara Evans also received a cursed letter and is now over on the mainland trying to save the post office from permanent closure.'

'*Achoo*!'

'Bless you, Mr Starr. But with Barbara not here to deliver any more post, the curse should hopefully spread no further.'

'You don't know that, though, do you, Mayor? The ghost might be able to spread this curse in other ways,' Mr Finch argued.

'And what do you intend to do to help those of us who have already been cursed?' asked Mr Potts.

'I will do my utmost to find a way of stopping the curse affecting those it currently is. If anyone has any ideas, please do share them with me.'

As everyone started talking again, Becky said to Jimmy, 'We need Spooky Steve – he'll be able to help.'

'But if he's been cursed and is really ill in bed, he won't be able to help, will he?' Jimmy pointed out.

Becky stood up. 'Well he'll just have to! I'm going to see him.'

Not So Spooky Steve

'It's not your fault. You didn't know a ghost was going to appear,' said Jimmy, struggling to keep up as Becky paced down Watersplash Lane.

'You saw them all staring at me in there. I was the one who invented a post office ghost and pulled that stupid prank in the spare room,' she replied. 'So I'm responsible for Walter Anion turning up. Now all these bad things are happening, because of me.'

They turned left onto the coastal path, heading for the White Wing. As they passed the harbour, Becky saw Albert sitting outside the harbour hut, staring at the ground. The old fisherman, whose very wrinkles showed the depth of the sea he sailed in, was unable to fish. His boat was firmly tied up and the barrels around the harbour stood empty. Even the seagulls had given up hope of finding fish, and were squabbling on the rocks.

'Poor Albert,' said Becky.

'You feel sorry for him, do you?' came a loud voice.

The children looked up. Striding along the path towards them was Finn.

'Yes,' Becky replied. 'I'm sorry for your granddad, and for Mr Starr and Mr Finch, and my mum and everyone else.'

'Well you should be sorry.' Finn towered over her, breathing heavily. 'It's all your fault. You said you'd get your own back on me, but I never thought you'd go this far, setting a ghost on us.'

'Becky didn't set the ghost on you. She didn't stop your granddad from fishing, either. How could she?' Jimmy said in a high-pitched voice. He stood in front of her and tried his best to stare Finn down.

For a minute, Finn looked like he was going to punch Jimmy, who started to tremble. Then Finn let out a long sigh and turned around.

'You're horrible, Becky Evans, that's what you are, horrible!' he called back to her.

'I'm sorry, Finn. I didn't mean for it to happen, I promise. The ghost, it … I don't know how it happened. I …'

Her voice faded away as she watched Finn walk over to Albert and put his arm around him.

'You see, Jimmy? It is my fault. I have to do something. I have to stop the curse. But how?'

'We're going to see Spooky Steve. That's a start,' said Jimmy.

'Yeah,' said Becky. 'If Spooky Steve is such a good ghost hunter, he'll know how to solve this.'

***

Ms Galway looked up from the crossword she was doing behind the bar. 'Sorry, Becky, I can't let anyone see Spooky Steve. He's very ill and I'm under orders from Dr Crystal.'

'Can you at least tell me which room he's staying in?' Becky pleaded.

'I'm afraid not, sorry.'

Becky turned away from the bar.

'What should we do now?' asked Jimmy.

Becky spotted a familiar face over in the corner, staring out at the sea. It was Carl, Spooky Steve's cameraman.

'Hello, you two,' he said in a friendly voice when they walked over to him. 'I've just been admiring the view. Thistlewick really is a beautiful place. Listen, I'm really sorry about the other night. That ghost was pretty terrifying, wasn't it? And it's terrible what's been happening since then.'

The children nodded.

'Anyway, where are my manners? Sit yourselves down.' They flopped into the comfy chairs opposite Carl. He was a lot more talkative without his director around. 'I've been working on *Hunting Ghosts* for three years now. You get used to seeing some pretty creepy things – like the stuff that happened with Little Lord Thistlewick's ghost. I don't usually get spooked by it, but that one at the post office …'

'Walter Anion,' Becky prompted.

'Walter Anion, well he was something else. Shook me right up. To see a ghost take the shape of a fully formed person in front of you is really rare. Most people, even ghost hunters like Steve, never see one.'

'Walter must be really angry to want to curse people,' said Becky.

Carl nodded. 'When they die, people only leave behind a ghost if they have unfinished business. All the ghosts we find in the show have something important they didn't achieve when they were alive, which they have to do as a ghost before they can settle. Quite often the ghosts we find are upset or angry. Maybe Walter Anion has a grudge against the post office.'

'What's going to happen to *Hunting Ghosts* now?' asked Jimmy.

The cameraman took a sip from his beer. 'Craig, my director, has been running around like a headless chicken. He wanted to leave Thistlewick the second we got out of the post office. He's arranged for a boat to take us back to the mainland in an hour or two. We're going to work on other projects while Steve's recovering.'

'What about Steve – will he go with you? Surely he's too ill to travel?' asked Becky.

'That's what he says,' Carl said doubtfully.

'Do you believe him? Do you think he was cursed, like he said the other night?'

'I'm not sure. Craig is quite easy to read. He's just a bully, as I'm sure you've seen. Like all bullies, as soon as something more threatening than him comes along, he wants to run away. But Steve is a bit of a mystery, and he's never reacted to a ghost like that before. There's something fishy going on with him.'

'I don't think it really makes sense, Steve being cursed,' Jimmy thought out loud. 'Everyone else who has been cursed received a letter. But Steve didn't get a letter, did he?'

'None of the rest of us who were in the room that night have been cursed, either,' said Becky.

'That's a good point,' said Carl. 'Do you know that it took a long time to persuade Steve to come to Thistlewick. Your mayor has been contacting the TV show for the last two years, but Steve has always been reluctant. In the end, Craig had to force him into it.'

'We really need to talk to Steve,' said Becky.

'What about? I can't claim to be an expert, but I've been on plenty of ghost hunts with Steve.' Carl looked over to the bar. Craig was there settling his bill with Ms Galway. 'I don't have long now, but maybe I can help.'

'We really need to stop the curse. Do you know of any ways we can do that?' asked Becky.

Carl weighed some thoughts up in his mind as he finished his drink. 'There is something I saw Steve do once, ages ago, with a particularly troublesome ghost.'

Becky and Jimmy leant forwards eagerly as Carl continued.

'You'll need to bring Walter Anion's ghost back, I'm afraid – you have to confront him again. But the problem is, it takes a phenomenal amount of energy for a ghost to form a shape as detailed as he's done. His energies will be very low.'

'What do you mean?' asked Jimmy.

'Ghosts and spirits work by taking energy from the environment around them and using it to create a presence that we can see and hear. That's why you often feel cold when you're around ghosts – they've sucked all the heat energy out of the place they're in. That means that you need to give Walter lots of energy to make him reappear. You can do that by holding a Calling.'

'What's that?' Becky was sitting at the edge of her seat.

Carl explained. A Calling involved a group of people standing in a circle in the dark, asking a ghost to appear.

'That seems a bit too easy,' said Becky.

'People have been doing it for centuries, and as I said, I've seen Steve doing it, so it can work. You'll need to get everyone who's been affected by the curse to come along to the Calling. They all have a connection with the ghost now, so the more cursed people there, the greater the chance of him showing up.'

'And what do we do once he's appeared?' asked Jimmy.

'You reverse the curse,' said Carl. 'This ghost is cursing all the letters in the post office, right? So I think if you write a letter to Walter Anion, it will be cursed like all the others. You can deliver the letter to him by placing it in the centre of the circle. Hopefully when he reads it he'll be defeated by his own curse, and that will cancel it out.'

Becky nodded. 'That sounds like a great idea. We'll give it a go when it gets dark tonight.'

The director walked over to them and glared at the children from under his baseball cap.

'Steve was right. It was a bad idea coming here – I'll be glad if I never see the place again. Carl, I don't pay you to talk to people, especially not these two. They've caused enough problems for us. Our boat's in, so let's get off this island.'

He stormed off. Carl smiled at Becky and Jimmy apologetically.

'I'll keep my fingers crossed that it works for you,' he said.

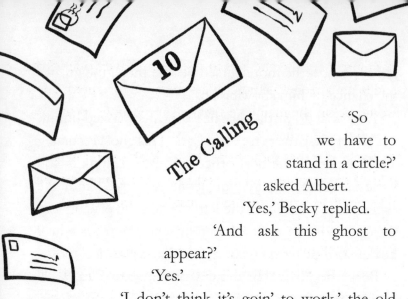

The Calling

'So we have to stand in a circle?' asked Albert.

'Yes,' Becky replied.

'And ask this ghost to appear?'

'Yes.'

'I don't think it's goin' to work,' the old fisherman mumbled.

'It's what Carl said we need to do. Walter Anion needs energy to appear, and he will use all our joint energy to do that,' said Becky.

'We have to give it *a … a … achoo …* a go, Albert. We have to try and stop this,' said Mr Starr, whose nose was looking ripe red. 'I'm not able to play my violin with this *achoo …* sneezing. I can't work!'

'I know, I know, I can't take it much longer without my fish,' said Albert.

'Right, it has to be as dark as possible,' said Becky.

She pulled the curtains shut and signalled to Jimmy to turn the light off.

'Now let's get into a circle and hold hands.'

There were over thirty people crowded into the small spare room, and they did as they were told, forming a tight circle around the bed in the centre. Everyone who had been cursed was there, apart from Becky's mum. She would be on the mainland by now, in meetings trying to save the post office.

Becky put that thought to the back of her mind, and placed the envelope addressed to Walter Anion on the bed. She had written the letter inside it earlier:

Dear Walter Anion,

Please read this carefully. The curse you have put on the post office is affecting so many people – it is horrible. I do not know why you are so angry, but please stop your curse and let everyone it has affected return to normal. Please leave the post office, and my mum, in peace.

Becky Evans

The letter in place, Becky moved back to the edge of the circle and held hands with Mr Starr and Jimmy.

She could tell that her friend was putting on a brave face. The thought of coming back into the spare room must have terrified him. She squeezed his hand.

'You're really brave, Jimmy. Far braver than Spooky Steve.'

Across the circle, Finn was glaring at her. She gulped.

'Who's going to ask this ghost to appear?' asked Mr Finch.

'Becky should,' said Finn. 'She's the one who set it on everyone.'

'Finn!' Albert snapped.

'OK …' Becky closed her eyes and gripped the hands on either side of her tightly. Then she began a speech, based on what Carl said Steve had spoken at the Calling he had done. 'Walter Anion, please come to us. I am here with all the people your curse has affected and we want you to appear at the centre of this circle. We have something important to give you. Please come to us.'

Becky paused. The room was silent, apart from a quiet sniff from Mr Starr. Carl said it would get cold if Walter turned up, and she couldn't feel any change in temperature.

'This is ridiculous,' Mr Finch said under his breath. Finn nodded in agreement.

That made Becky even more determined that the Calling would work. She continued, 'Use our joint energies to appear in the centre of the circle. We have a letter for you. Please come and read it.'

'Did you feel that?' asked Mr Potts.

Becky opened her eyes. 'What?'

'I did. My legs feel cold,' said Jimmy, gripping Becky's hand even tighter. 'There's a breeze around them.'

'Put some proper clothes on, then, instead of those stupid shorts,' said Finn.

'I feel it too,' said Albert in barely a whisper.

'If that was you, Walter Anion, you're doing the right thing. Please move into the centre of the circle,' said Becky.

She suddenly felt a dramatic drop in the temperature of the room – in the temperature of her own body. It was like all the heat – all the energy – was being sucked out of her. The Calling was working!

The breeze around everyone's legs started to rise up. Behind Becky, the curtains blew wildly. A large gust of wind blew through the room. People around the circle gasped.

Jimmy's grip on Becky's hand was becoming unbearable. She saw Albert opposite her – his eyes were wide open, his teeth gritted in his mouth, his beard twitching. Others around the circle were starting to fidget nervously.

'Find the letter, Walter Anion, find it and read it,' Becky said loudly.

Mr Starr gave a sharp intake of breath and broke his hand away from the circle to point.

'You … you need to keep holding onto Becky's hand, Mr Starr,' Jimmy called to him.

But Becky looked at where he was pointing, to the letter on the bed. Slowly, it started to rise up in the air. Was Walter Anion picking it up?

As the letter rose up and up, it began shaking madly. No one seemed sure what to do. Was this what was meant

to happen? Was the ghost going to open the envelope?

Suddenly it stopped shaking. Then Becky saw with dismay that a hole had appeared in the middle of the envelope, like it had been burnt through. Smoke started billowing from its edges.

Becky broke the circle and ran forwards – this wasn't right.

'Becky, be careful!' called Mr Potts.

Halfway to the bed she froze. The letter burst into bright orange flames and in a flash it had turned to blackened ashes, which blasted straight at her.

There was a shattering scream – a man's scream – so loud that the room shook.

Even as she covered her ears, Becky couldn't mistake what it was shouting.

'Noooooooo!'

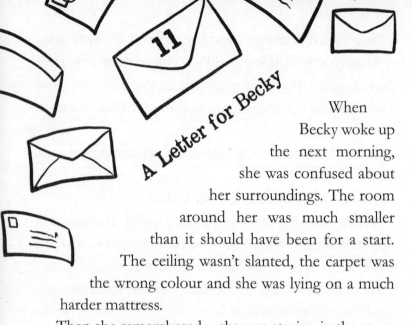

11

A Letter for Becky

When Becky woke up the next morning, she was confused about her surroundings. The room around her was much smaller than it should have been for a start. The ceiling wasn't slanted, the carpet was the wrong colour and she was lying on a much harder mattress.

Then she remembered – she was staying in the spare room at Jimmy's house.

She got up and wandered over to the window. The sky outside was grey and overcast, threatening rain, which suited her mood perfectly. The view from her room looked out over the market square, and she saw the post office with a big 'Closed Until Further Notice' sign on the door, and her home above it, all dark and empty.

They must have really annoyed Walter Anion for him to have reacted like he did, setting the letter on fire. She was half worried that he would try to make his curse get even worse, but at least now that no post was going in or out of the post office, he wouldn't be able to do it that way.

There was a knock at the door; Jimmy's mum poked her head around it. 'Morning, Becky, your mum's on the phone.'

Becky ran down the stairs to the phone in the hallway. 'Mum?'

'Hello, love.' She sounded tired, but Becky realised how much she missed her.

'It's so good to hear your voice, Mum!'

Becky spent most of the conversation listening to what had been going on in Mum's meetings on the mainland. It didn't sound good. The postal service seemed determined that they were going to close the Thistlewick post office. If that happened, Becky and Mum would have to move out of their flat. Mum asked lots of questions about what was happening on Thistlewick, but Becky did her best to avoid answering them. She didn't want to worry her, or risk her getting angry. But by the end of the conversation, Becky knew her time to stop the curse was limited – Mum only had a few more days of meetings before the postal service made their final decision. Becky just knew that if she did manage to stop the curse, everything would end positively.

As she put the phone down, Jimmy's mum wandered over looking puzzled.

'I thought there wasn't meant to be any post now?' she asked.

'There isn't, Mrs Cole.'

'Well that's most odd, because I found this on the doormat.' Jimmy's mum held out a brown envelope. 'It's addressed to you, Becky.'

Becky stared at the old-fashioned, spiky handwriting:

Becky Evans
The Spare Room
Number Ten Market Square
Thistlewick

'I don't think I should touch it,' she mumbled. 'Please can you throw it in the bin?'

Her legs shook as she climbed back up the stairs.

The curse will get worse, she thought.

***

'Jimmy, Jimmy. Open your door!' Becky banged on his bedroom door.

It slowly opened.

'What is it?' Jimmy said with a yawn.

'Did you get a letter too?' she asked, forcing her way in and sitting down on the bed.

'No, of course I didn't get a letter,' he replied. 'What do you mean?'

'It must just be me, then. Walter Anion is mad at me, so he's trying to curse me.'

'You got a letter?' Panic spread across Jimmy's face. Becky nodded.

'What did you do with it?'

'Your mum threw it in the bin.'

'Good.' He gave a sigh of relief.

'But the point is, Jimmy, he was able to send the letter. Even with the post office closed, he's still able to make his curse worse. I have to stop him, but I … I just don't know what to do.'

Fists clenched, she stared out of the window at the mist rolling in from the sea.

'Let's be logical about it,' said Jimmy. 'What do we know about Walter Anion?'

Becky turned around. 'We've been through this. We don't know anything about him. Just that he's an angry ghost.'

'And why would an angry ghost turn up in your spare room four days ago and start cursing things?'

'Because I pretended there was a ghost. Oh, it's all my fault!' Becky said in frustration.

'That's not the reason he turned up, Becky.' Then Jimmy's eyes lit up. 'But what if he did appear because of someone in the room that night? Maybe he's connected to one of us!'

'It can't be me or you, can it?' asked Becky. 'We'd never heard of Walter Anion.'

'Plus we've been in your spare room loads of times

before. But could he be connected to Spooky Steve, or Carl, or Craig, in some way?'

'I bet you it's Steve. Remember what Carl said about him not wanting to come to Thistlewick?'

'We don't really know much about him, do we?' said Jimmy.

'Then it's about time we investigated Spooky Steve,' said Becky.

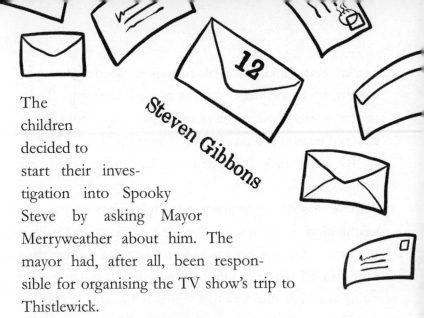

The children decided to start their investigation into Spooky Steve by asking Mayor Merryweather about him. The mayor had, after all, been responsible for organising the TV show's trip to Thistlewick.

When they got to the island hall, they found Mayor Merryweather standing on the stage, shouting directions to Mr Morris, who was in charge of Thistlewick's pest control.

'To your left, Mr Morris. No, in the far corner. You almost had it. There's another to your right. There are so many of the blighters!'

Mr Morris was running back and forth swinging a net across the floor.

'Oh, hello, children,' the mayor called, seeing Becky and Jimmy in the entrance. 'Do come in, but be careful where you stand. We have a rat infestation. That's it, straight ahead of you, Mr Morris … you nearly had it that time.'

'Don't you use poison to get rid of rats?' asked Jimmy.

Having no luck at all, Mr Morris stopped and looked angrily at the children. As she moved forwards, Becky saw why. His curse was a particularly nasty one. He was covered in sore looking bites, all over his face and arms.

'It's ever since I opened that blooming letter you delivered, telling me I would be inspected by the pest control board,' he explained to her. 'My poison's not working on them, and my traps are all faulty. I'm having to use this medieval method to try and catch them. But every time I try, they bite me and run away. They keep biting through my nets too – this is the third one I've used in two days.'

'You'll just have to leave it, Mr Morris,' said the mayor. 'Is there anything I can do to ease the problem?'

'There's not much I can suggest. They used arsenic in the old days, and that worked well enough, but it's not considered safe any more. Arsenic doesn't just affect the rats you see – it poisons other animals and people too. You really need to sort this curse out, Mayor Merryweather. I cannot do my job properly when I can't catch rats. My inspection is next week and I'll fail it at this rate. Even worse, if we're not careful, Thistlewick is going to be infested with rodents!'

'We're doing our best to stop the curse, Mr Morris,' the mayor replied calmly.

Mr Morris sighed and limped off.

Mayor Merryweather turned to the children. 'I'm

sure we'll figure out what to do in the next few days. We used to have a ghost hunter called Eric, who lived on Thistlewick, you know.'

'Used to? What happened to him?' asked Becky.

'He went missing about ten years ago.'

'Missing?' asked Jimmy.

'No one really knows what happened. It was all quite a mystery. One day he walked into the forest in search of ghosts and he never returned. Anyway, Eric used to keep a record of his methods in a book, so I'll see if I can find that. But what is it I can do for you now, children?'

Becky watched a rat dash straight past them and into a hole under the stage. 'We were hoping you could tell us a bit about Spooky Steve.'

'Truth be told, I can't say I know a lot about him, other than what we have seen from TV. Why don't we have a look on the interweb?' His eyes lit up as he said this – any excuse to use a computer got Mayor Merryweather excited. 'There'll be some information on Spooky Steve's web-thingy, I expect.'

'Website,' Jimmy corrected.

They followed the mayor through to his office behind the stage. He shut the door to stop any of the rats getting in and loaded up his computer.

'Now what was the address-thingy?' the mayor thought out loud. 'I had it written down somewhere.'

He started sifting through the papers on his desk.

'It's www dot spookysteve dot co dot uk,' said Becky.

Mayor Merryweather slowly typed the address into the computer and the website started to load.

'The interweb's being very slow today. Let's hope it's not a pesky seagull biting through the phone lines again.'

Six floating ghosts appeared on the screen, and Becky showed Mayor Merryweather how to click on them to load the different pages. He was aiming for 'Biography', but accidentally clicked on 'Photo Gallery' and 'Press Kit' before getting to the right page. Staring out of the screen at them was an image of Steve's face, which changed every five seconds, first showing a broad grin, then his trademark spooky look.

Mayor Merryweather started to read out the biography. 'Spooky Steve, the world famous ghost hunter and presenter of *Hunting Ghosts with Spooky Steve*, has a special gift for attracting the supernatural. Christened Steven Gibbons, it all started when he saw his first ghost aged seven – the ghost of his recently deceased pet hamster, Nibbles.'

'Hang on, why do I recognise the name Gibbons?' asked Becky.

'I know!' said Jimmy. 'I've been doing some research on the Thistlewick family since that night on Barefoot Bay. Little Lord Thistlewick's sister, Coral-Anne, married a man called Grinlin Gibbons.'

'Yes, that's true, Jimmy, well done,' said the mayor.

'Grinlin Gibbons is a creepy name. Does that mean Spooky Steve is related to Lord Thistlewick?' asked Becky.

The mayor smiled. 'That was my first thought. I asked him about it when we were discussing his coming to Thistlewick. He said it is just a coincidence that he has that surname.'

'Hmmm ...' said Becky. 'There have been too many coincidences with Steve. Like it can't have just been a coincidence that Walter Anion's ghost turned up and threatened Steve when he did. Steven Gibbons is hiding something, and I think he's a member of the Thistlewick family.'

'But still, how does that link him to Walter Anion?' asked Jimmy.

'I don't know,' Becky admitted.

'I agree that something doesn't quite add up with Spooky Steve, but saying he is a descendant of Lord Thistlewick is quite a big jump to make,' said Mayor Merryweather.

'Mayor!' came a call from the hall.

They all walked out of the mayor's office to find Finn standing by the stage, out of breath.

'Oh, it's you two,' he said, glaring at Becky and Jimmy as if they were just two more rats running around on the floor.

'What is it, Finn?' the mayor asked.

'It's Granddad,' Finn replied. 'He's so upset by this curse stuff that he's refusing to get out of bed. Can you come and talk to him?'

'I'll come straight away,' said Mayor Merryweather. He turned to Becky and Jimmy. 'Sorry, you two, I must go and help Albert.'

***

Jimmy took Becky to the library to show her the research he'd done on Lord Thistlewick.

In *The Thistlewick Family: An Intimate Biography* there were small paintings of the Thistlewicks: the large, powerful Lord Thistlewick in his purple cloak – Becky had seen lots of images of him before; his smart son, Little Lord Thistlewick, standing by a silky horse; Lord Thistlewick's daughter, Coral-Anne, wearing a black dress and looking beautiful with long, wavy hair. The description under her painting said she was wearing black because it was painted while she was mourning the loss of her brother.

'I'm sure I've seen Coral-Anne Thistlewick before,' said Becky.

'Another painting of her is hanging up at the White Wing,' said Jimmy. 'You've probably seen that.'

There were two theories about what had caused Little Lord Thistlewick's fatal fall from his horse on his tenth birthday, according to the book. Some people thought he had lost control of the horse, others thought that the horse had been poisoned and fallen, taking the young Lord down with it.

The book went on to detail the marriage of Coral-Anne Thistlewick to Lord Grinlin Gibbons about a year after her brother's death.

Becky was sure that Steve was a descendant of Grinlin and Coral-Anne, and therefore of Lord Thistlewick. Jimmy was right, though – that still didn't give a connection between Steve and the ghost of Walter Anion.

They traipsed back to Jimmy's house that evening feeling frustrated.

'Becky,' said a flustered Mrs Cole as they sat down for dinner. 'This has just turned up for you.'

She held out a brown envelope.

'Another letter?' Becky groaned.

'Shall I throw this one in the bin too?' asked Mrs Cole.

'Yes, please,' said Becky. 'And if any more come, throw them away too.'

***

Why can't you just leave me alone! Becky shouted in her mind to Walter Anion, wherever he was. *I'm not opening your letters, so you can't put your stupid curse on me!*

The shouts in her mind were interrupted by real ones coming from outside. She peered out of the bedroom window. The stall owners in the market square were mostly packing up for the night. The noise was coming from the farm stall, where a battle of words was taking place.

Mr Potts stood there helplessly as Mr Finch spoke rudely to Mrs Didsbury. 'I got to the stall first. It's mine by rights.'

'Nonsense,' Mrs Didsbury replied shrilly. 'I had my hand on it before you even came close.'

It sounded like they were arguing about something really important, but as Becky craned her neck she saw a solitary bottle of milk on the table in front of Mr Potts. With his cows ill, the poor farmer was no longer able to produce milk, and this looked like it was his last bottle. Things must really be bad if people were fighting over milk.

'Why don't you share it?' Mr Potts was attempting to say.

'I need it for my tea,' Mr Finch spoke over him.

'Well I have weak bones,' argued Mrs Didsbury. 'I think my health is more important than your *tea*! And may I remind you, Braden Finch, that you still owe me a chair, which I have already paid for. You should buy the milk for me out of that money.'

'It's not my fault I can't use a saw any more. It's that

retched post office curse. Give me the milk, Andrew.'

'No, I'll take it,' said Mrs Didsbury.

They all stopped, however, when they saw Mr Morris running straight at them, waving a net. A rat jumped up onto Mr Potts's stall and before anyone could do anything, Mr Morris's net had caught the bottle. It fell to the ground and smashed, sending the milk gushing out. The rat, which Mr Morris had failed to catch, squeaked, gave him a bite and started licking up the milk.

'I'm so sorry,' said Mr Morris.

'Thistlewick is falling apart!' Mr Finch exclaimed, turning away and glaring at the post office.

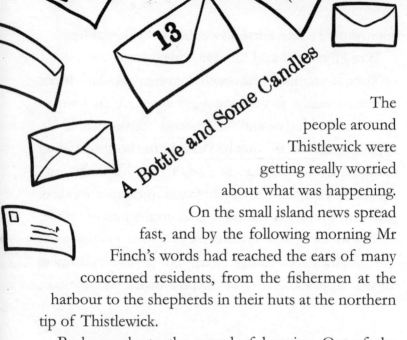

13
A Bottle and Some Candles

The people around Thistlewick were getting really worried about what was happening. On the small island news spread fast, and by the following morning Mr Finch's words had reached the ears of many concerned residents, from the fishermen at the harbour to the shepherds in their huts at the northern tip of Thistlewick.

Becky awoke to the sound of banging. Out of the window she saw a group of islanders gathered in the market. She rubbed her eyes and saw with horror what they were doing – hammering planks of wood onto the post office!

She threw on her dressing gown and ran down the stairs and out of the house.

'What are you doing?!' she called.

It was a group of ten men, including Mr Potts, Mr Morris and Finn. But it was Mr Finch who was giving the orders. They had covered the two post office windows in wood and were halfway through boarding up the front door.

'Finn, take this piece of wood to Mr Potts, would

you?' said Mr Finch, handing him a badly cut plank.

Becky ran over to Finn and ripped the wood out of his hands. She pushed through the men and tried to tear the wood from the windows.

'Stop it!' she shouted. 'Why are you doing this?'

'I'm sorry, Becky, after the Calling failed we had to try something. Things have got so bad,' said Mr Potts.

Mr Finch walked over. 'I may not be able to carve properly, but at least I can put my wood to some use. My old man always said that the only thing ghosts can't get through is wood, so we're trapping Walter Anion in the post office. If he can't escape, he can't curse us any more.'

Becky shook her head in disbelief. Nothing she could say would stop them. She ran to fetch Mayor Merryweather.

He was looking through a small black book in his office when she burst in. She explained what was happening and he came straight to the market.

'Stop this at once!' he demanded, puffing out his chest.

Mr Finch turned. 'With respect, Mayor, why should we? You're not doing anything to stop the curse. Carry on boarding the place up, men.'

'Ghosts not being able to get through wood? I've never heard anything so foolish,' said Mayor Merryweather.

'If you have any better ideas, now's your time to tell

us,' said Mr Finch, hammering a fresh piece of wood over the door.

'With all the power I have on Thistlewick Island, I command you to cease this nonsense! Do as your mayor says!' Mayor Merryweather boomed.

The men dropped their tools. Mr Finch looked like he was going to say something nasty.

'This isn't over. We'll be back!' He stormed out of the market.

'Thank you,' Becky said to the mayor.

A pleasant sound came into the market, diffusing the tension. It was Mr Starr, playing his violin.

'But Mr Starr, I thought your cold meant you couldn't play ...' Becky began.

The musician beamed at her. 'It seems I was wrong, Becky. It seems I haven't been cursed at all.'

'What do you mean, Isaac?' asked the mayor.

'When I returned home and found the parcel in my letter box, I never actually opened it. I brought it straight to the island meeting, where you explained about the cursed post, and I just assumed I had been cursed like all the others. But I began wondering what was in the parcel, and last night curiosity got the better of me. I opened it to find nothing malicious, just medicine for colds. I took the medicine last night, and by this morning my sneezing had stopped. Turns out it was just an ordinary cold. I can play my violin again!'

'But I definitely delivered that parcel to you the same day as all the other cursed post. It has to have been cursed,' said Becky.

'It seems not,' Mr Starr replied. 'In fact, it's almost as if someone decided to help me from afar. I hadn't ordered any cold medicine, and there was no clue in the parcel about who it was from.'

'It's a mystery,' the mayor commented.

'Good day to you.' Mr Starr practically skipped away, playing a merry tune as he went.

Becky stared after him, confused. It didn't make any sense.

'I have some good news of my own, Becky,' said Mayor Merryweather. 'I think I have found a way for us to try and sort out the Walter problem.'

She looked up hopefully. 'What is it?'

'I found Eric's notebook. There's only really one method that will work, according to his notes. It's a very old method that he used once or twice with problem ghosts. Why don't you fetch Jimmy and meet me back here in ten minutes. We'll need a glass bottle with a cork if you can find one.'

***

Mayor Merryweather, Becky and Jimmy positioned themselves around the bedside cabinet in Becky's spare room.

Becky rubbed her hands in anticipation. 'What's the plan?'

'We're going to try to bottle Walter Anion,' said the mayor.

Jimmy frowned. 'Bottle him?'

'That's right. Do you have the corked bottle?'

Becky handed the mayor an empty wine bottle that Jimmy's mum had been throwing out when she'd asked for one. He placed it on top of the cabinet.

'Now we need four candles.'

He removed some from his pocket and gave them to Jimmy.

'Place them evenly around the bottle,' he instructed.

Jimmy carefully arranged them, and the mayor struck a match and lit each one in turn. The flames flickered for a moment then settled into steady points of light.

With the curtains drawn, Becky thought the candle-light highlighting the mayor's and Jimmy's faces made them look really creepy.

'How are we going get him into the bottle?' asked Becky.

'It won't be dangerous, will it?' asked Jimmy.

'Not according to Eric. I am just following his instructions. Jimmy, hold the bottle steady. If it starts to shake, don't let it fall over. Becky, keep an eye out for a blue light – that will be Walter taking the heat from the candles.'

Mayor Merryweather took a deep breath and leant forwards.

'Rest, spirit, rest,' he said.

The room around them was in dead silence. Nothing moved.

'Well he's definitely resting,' said Jimmy nervously. 'Nothing happened.'

'Jimmy, ssshhh!' said Becky. She focussed intensely on the candles as the mayor continued.

'Take the energy from our candles. It's all for you, Walter Anion.'

The two candles on Becky's side of the cabinet flickered wildly and with a flash of blue went out. She gasped and felt Jimmy grab her hand.

'Hold on to the bottle, Jimmy,' she reminded him. 'Does the blue light mean he's here?'

'Yes, and we've got his attention,' said the mayor. 'Eric says the ghost will find the energy from the candles irresistible. He should now float into the centre of the candles, so he can enjoy all their energy at once.'

They waited. Becky gritted her teeth.

'Come on, Walter,' she muttered.

A small draught whisked around them and another candle went out.

'How are we going to know if Walter goes into the bottle?' Becky asked.

'Just keep looking for the blue light. If it all goes to

plan, he will be sucked down into the bottle and it will glow blue,' said the mayor. 'Come on, make your move.'

The final candle flame reached up, tall and thin. It changed to an intense blue colour.

'Look,' said Becky. 'Look!'

Then it vanished. The room plunged into darkness. Mayor Merryweather walked away from the cabinet.

Becky looked round anxiously. 'Did it work?'

'We came so close, but sadly not. The bottle isn't glowing blue, and when all the candles go out, that is the end of it.'

'Could we try again?' asked Jimmy.

'He won't fall for the same trick twice,' said the mayor. 'My instructions say that you only really get one shot at it.'

'I can't believe we got so close!' Becky groaned.

***

When they stepped out of the post office, ducking under the wood panels that covered the top half of the entrance, they saw Mr Finch walking determinedly over to them.

Becky braced herself for his anger.

'We've been talking,' he said, but his voice wasn't angry, it was cold and calculating, which was possibly scarier, 'me and a group of the others who are affected by this curse. We have a new plan.'

'And that is?' Mayor Merryweather asked sceptically.

'We think the most effective way to get rid of the ghost is to destroy the post office. Knock it down. Without it, Walter Anion's curse will be nothing.'

'No, you can't!' Becky burst out. 'It's my home!'

'For goodness' sake, are you thinking straight, man, or has the curse affected your mind too?' said the mayor. 'Knock down the post office! Don't be so ridiculous.'

Mr Finch glared at them and spoke as if he was reading from a script. 'I implore you to consult the Thistlewick code of practice and demand that code three is put into action.'

Becky frowned and asked Mayor Merryweather, 'What does he mean?'

The mayor's eyes never left Mr Finch as he talked. 'It is a law of Thistlewick that any person wishing for something to happen has the right to put it to a vote of the people of Thistlewick. Mr Finch is demanding that we vote on whether the post office should be knocked down.'

'Well I vote that it shouldn't!' Becky shouted.

'Me too!' Jimmy seconded.

'That isn't how it works,' said Mr Finch. 'Shall I prepare the document, Mayor? Then we can see what everyone else thinks.'

'You do that,' the mayor replied gravely.

***

Lying in bed in Jimmy's spare room, Becky felt like a big ball of panic, rolling down a never-ending hill of worry.

So many bad things had happened in such a short space of time. On the phone that night, Mum sounded like she had no energy left; over on the mainland she was doing all she could to save her livelihood. Becky would now have to fight to save the post office on Thistlewick. Mayor Merryweather had told her not to be concerned – there was not a chance that people would vote to knock down the post office; it was just Mr Finch being a fool.

After everything that had gone on already, though, Becky couldn't feel as confident as the mayor.

She knew it was all up to her now. The mayor had tried his best, but Walter's ghost wasn't having any of it. Becky had to stop the curse. She was sure that if she could just figure out the reason for Walter's ghost turning up in the first place, that might help.

Becky fell into an uneasy sleep. It wasn't long before she saw the familiar vision of the beautiful woman's face. Her eyes were still as blue as the sky on the best day of summer. The wind gently ran its fingers through her hair.

What are you trying to show me? Becky thought.

The image changed. Now there was a different picture of the woman. This time she was with a young, tall man.

They looked happy, smiling into each other's eyes.

I recognise both of you, Becky thought. *But who are you?*

Around the man's neck was a brown bag, the same as Becky used for delivering the post. She saw his green eyes. It was Walter, from when he was a much younger man.

But where had she seen the woman?

She thought back to the paintings in *The Thistlewick Family: An Intimate Biography* ...

Becky shook herself awake. She suddenly realised – the visions she'd been having were of Coral-Anne Thistlewick, who she suspected was Spooky Steve's ancestor. And now she had seen a vision of Coral-Anne with Walter Anion – Becky had found the connection between Steve and the ghost!

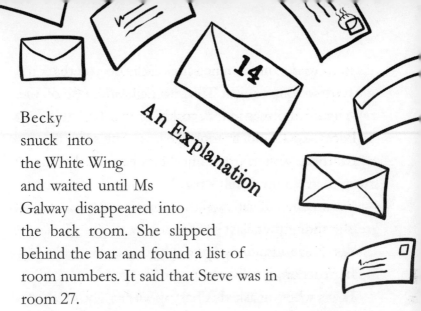

An Explanation

Becky snuck into the White Wing and waited until Ms Galway disappeared into the back room. She slipped behind the bar and found a list of room numbers. It said that Steve was in room 27.

She climbed the stairs to the rooms quietly and crept past all the other numbers until she got to room 27. Becky knocked on the door.

'Is that you, Ms Galway? Could you fetch me some more water?' came a familiar voice.

Becky opened the door and found Steve slouched in the chair by the window, reading a newspaper. He didn't look ill at all.

'You didn't tell the truth!' she blurted out, more aggressively than she had intended.

'Becky … what are you doing here?'

'Why didn't you say that you're part of the Thistlewick family?' she demanded.

'You found out …' Steve looked shocked for a few seconds, then sat up. 'There's no point in keeping it secret now, I suppose. *Hunting Ghosts with Spooky Steve* has been going on for nine series. Why do you think it's taken us so long to visit Thistlewick Island, one of the most haunted places in the world?'

'I don't know,' Becky replied.

'I've been avoiding coming here, because I've been trying to avoid my family's past.'

'Coral-Anne Thistlewick is your great-great-great-great-grandmother, isn't she?'

'Yes,' Steve admitted. 'Although you need to add a few more greats on. She lived a long time ago.'

'That's why you asked Albert about her ghost?'

'And I think it's why her brother appeared to me so strongly on Barefoot Bay. He realised our connection.'

'So what's your connection to Walter Anion?' Becky asked.

'None. I do not have anything to do with him,' he said quickly.

'Yes you do.' Becky moved towards Steve. 'While you've been tucked up in here, I've been having visions of Walter with Coral-Anne Thistlewick. She was connected with him in some way, and because you're her descendant, you must be connected to him too.'

Steve sighed. 'Craig was wrong about you. You're a very clever girl, Becky, I see that now. I can't hide anything from you, can I?'

'No, because that's all you've been doing – hiding up here while Walter Anion has been doing so much damage to Thistlewick. And you haven't been cursed, have you? Look at you, you're fine.'

'Becky, I was so shocked that night. I honestly don't know if I have been cursed, but the shock affected me badly.'

'You're a ghost hunter. You're used to seeing ghosts. Why should you be shocked?'

'I was shocked because it wasn't just Walter Anion who recognised me. I recognised him too.'

Steve went over to his bedside drawer, took something out and handed it to her. It was a print of a painting. In it were Coral-Anne and Walter – in exactly the same position Becky had seen in her vision.

'If Walter was a friend of your ancestor, why did he try to strangle you, Steve? And why did he put a curse on the post office?'

'He was an evil man,' Steve replied in a harsh voice.

'But he was friends with Coral-Anne,' Becky persisted.

'That's what she thought. In fact they were more than friends – they were going to be married. But he betrayed her. He showed his true, horrible colours.'

'If you knew he was like that, why did you agree to go near the post office?' Becky asked.

'Walter Anion was just a name. I didn't know what job he had or where he'd lived, until his ghost turned up, Becky.'

She frowned at Steve, puzzled.

'You've tried to do some research on Walter Anion, haven't you?' he asked, reading her expression. 'And you've hardly found anything?'

'Yes, that's right.'

'That's because Lord Thistlewick had Walter Anion removed from the island records and books – any link that man had to Coral-Anne was erased. Until that night in the post office, I didn't know that he'd been the postmaster.'

Becky realised she hadn't breathed for quite a while – the more she talked to Steve, the more questions she had for him.

'What did Walter do that was so bad? Why did Lord Thistlewick write him out of the records?'

'Do you really want to know the truth?'

'Yes!'

'Walter Anion poisoned Little Lord Thistlewick's horse. He is responsible for the boy's death.'

Becky blinked. It took a few seconds for what Steve had just said to sink in.

'Steve, I'm sorry.'

'It's fine, Becky. It was a long time ago, and you didn't know.'

'But why would Walter want to poison Little Lord Thistlewick's horse if he was going to marry Coral-Anne? It doesn't make sense,' she said.

'We'll never know exactly. It is a story that has been

kept in secret by my family for centuries. My ancestors were too ashamed that Coral-Anne had fallen in love with a man who ended up a murderer to let the full details be recorded. Now it is all very vague. All I know is that Walter Anion was evil. A man named Lord Grinlin Gibbons discovered that it was him who had poisoned the horse. Grinlin informed Lord Thistlewick, and Walter was arrested. He was sentenced to life imprisonment and Coral-Anne never saw him again. She was devastated.'

'Coral-Anne married Grinlin Gibbons a year after her brother's death,' Becky remembered.

Steve nodded. 'That's right. He helped her to get over the tragedy, and soon they fell in love and married. They moved away from Thistlewick Island together after their first child was born and never returned, so Walter Anion was quickly forgotten. I am the first Gibbons to set foot on Thistlewick since they left.'

'And now Walter's ghost is being horrible again,' said Becky.

'A person's ghost carries the same emotions they had when they died. In Walter Anion's case, he was evil, so he's probably angry at me and Thistlewick.'

'You have to stop his curse, Steve. Mr Finch is threatening to knock down the post office!'

'I'm sorry to hear that, Becky, but I can't go back there again. I really can't. It would only make things worse,' said Steve.

'But you can't just hide up here. We need your help!' Becky pleaded.

'Well, there is something I can do ...'

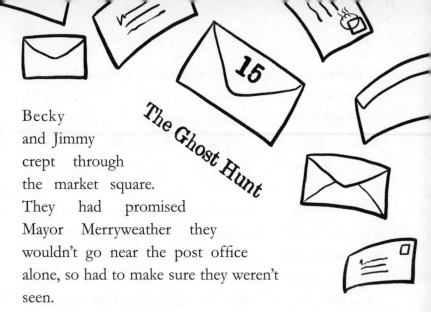

The Ghost Hunt

Becky and Jimmy crept through the market square. They had promised Mayor Merryweather they wouldn't go near the post office alone, so had to make sure they weren't seen.

Fortunately, it was mid-Monday morning and the market was very quiet, with only three stalls open and even fewer customers.

Mr Finch had attached an official-looking document to the post office door, calling for the destruction of the building, with a space underneath to write your name in a 'for' or 'against' column. The voting was to take place over the next two days. Becky panicked when she saw that out of the twenty people who had voted so far, there were ten votes in each column, meaning half the people wanted the post office to be knocked down. She and Jimmy added their names in big bold letters to the 'against' column and hoped more people would do the same.

'We have to figure out how to stop the curse before the votes are counted,' said Becky.

Inside, they climbed up the spiral staircase from the post office to the flat. Becky undid the lock on the flat's door and it creaked open. The only light was a thin beam coming through the cracks in the curtains, which were pulled across the windows. Becky wasn't used to her home being so dark.

Looking down, she saw some familiar objects on the welcome mat. She picked up the ten brown envelopes.

'They're all addressed to you,' said Jimmy.

For a minute, Becky actually found it hard not to open one. She couldn't help wondering what was inside – what *her* curse would be.

'Focus, Becky,' Jimmy reminded her.

'Yes,' she said. 'Steve says we need to try to talk directly to Walter. Then he might tell us why he's cursing people.'

'We're not going to have to try and make him appear like we did at the Calling, are we?'

'No, that didn't exactly go to plan, did it?' said Becky. 'Steve said his energy levels will be really low again.'

'So he won't be able to produce a full body apparition?' asked Jimmy.

'Er … what do you mean?' asked Becky.

'That he won't be able to appear looking like a human, like he did the first time.'

'Oh, right, yes,' said Becky, taken aback. 'Since when did you know about full body apparitions?'

'There are some links on Steve's website to information

about ghost hunting. I've been reading up on it.'

'You do like reading, don't you? We're going to talk to Walter using some special equipment Steve's given me. But I suppose you knew that already?'

'Yep.'

Becky took two black objects the size of calculators out of her bag.

'First we need to scan around using these, apparently,' said Becky, turning one around in her hand uncertainly.

'Electromagnetic field detectors,' said Jimmy.

'Electromag ... what?'

'Just call them EMFs. They detect the kind of energy that ghosts use.' Jimmy really did sound like he was reciting from a ghost-hunting handbook. 'That energy is spread all around us normally, but if there's a ghost present then there'll be a larger amount of it. We need to use these to find where Walter is hiding. Just wave it around like this.'

Jimmy took one of the devices and moved it along the wall in the hallway. A number came up on its screen – 0.7.

'If the number is lower than one, it's just a normal EMF reading, but if it's greater than one, that might be the place Walter is hiding. Does that make sense?' asked Jimmy.

'Yes, boss,' said Becky. She had a feeling that Jimmy was enjoying being in charge for once. 'Why don't you start scanning around my bedroom, I'll scan the spare room.'

Becky went in to the dimly lit spare room. She took an initial scan of the whole room and the detector read 0.8. She walked straight over to the rocking chair, where she had last seen Walter. Holding her breath in anticipation, she moved the reader up close to the wood. It beeped and a number flickered on the screen.

0.6 – that was disappointing.

The bed gave the same reading and the wardrobe gave 0.9. Becky went over to the bedside cabinet and looked at the drawer in it. Could ghosts hide in drawers? She tried scanning inside. 0.6 again.

Next she tried the wall by the window.

'6.5! Whoa! Jimmy, come and look at this.'

Jimmy ran into the room. 'Wow!'

He held his detector up against the wall. It read 6.5 too.

'Hello, Walter!' Becky exclaimed.

'Hang on, we need to be absolutely certain this means he is here,' said Jimmy.

'Of course it does,' said Becky.

'The only things other than ghosts that give off such high EMF reading are electrical equipment and plug sock … oh.'

Jimmy pointed to the wall. Just below Becky's EMF detector, there was a plug socket.

'So it's not Walter?' asked Becky.

'No.'

'Just a plug socket?'

'Yes …'

They continued scanning around the flat. It took hours! They tried to be as thorough as possible, scanning every corner of every room. They even went down to the post office sorting room (where Becky found several more letters addressed to her), but all the time the EMF readings were coming up as normal.

'That was a frustrating few hours,' said Jimmy.

'A complete waste of time,' Becky agreed. 'And look, it's nearly teatime.'

'We need to go back home soon, before my mum gets suspicious.'

'OK, let's just assume Walter is in the spare room,' said Becky. 'We'll move on to stage two, using this tape recorder.'

'So we're stopping EMF to do EVP?' asked Jimmy.

'What does EVP stand for, brain box? Electric violin playing?'

Jimmy frowned at her. 'Electronic voice phenomenon, actually.'

'Well that's a mouthful,' said Becky. 'We're going to try to get him to talk to us, if that's what you mean.'

They made their way to the spare room and sat down on the bed. Becky took out the tape recorder, which had a big microphone on the end of it.

'You hold the recorder, Jimmy, and I'll ask the questions.'

Jimmy pressed record and the EVP session began.

'Walter, this is Becky and Jimmy. We don't want to threaten you, we want to talk to you. Can you please tell us if you are here by talking into the tape recorder?'

Becky left a short pause and waited in silence. There was nothing that sounded like a reply, so she moved on to the next question.

'We want to understand why you are angry. Please could you tell us?'

She waited again. Still nothing.

'Are you hearing anything, Jimmy?'

'No, but you need to leave longer pauses between your questions,' he replied.

'Why? It's not like Walter is saying anything.'

'We don't know that,' Jimmy persisted. 'We won't actually be able to hear him speaking now, but the recorder is much better at picking up sounds than our ears. When we listen back to this on tape, it might have been able to record his voice.'

Becky wasn't positive that it would work, but she kept going. 'We think that you're angry because of something to do with Coral-Anne Thistlewick. Is that correct?'

This time she left a thirty-second pause.

'And does it have something to do with Little Lord Thistlewick, as well?'

Although there was silence after this question, Becky was suddenly aware of an uneasy feeling in her chest. She ignored it and kept going.

'Why did you poison Little Lord Thistlewick's horse, Walter?'

Ten seconds later, the uneasy feeling in Becky's chest increased, so rapidly that she gasped. Beside her, Jimmy was trembling.

'Becky, can we stop now? I need to get out of here.'

***

Out in the corridor, they both breathed in deeply.

'What happened in there?' asked Jimmy.

'I don't know,' Becky replied. 'Let's play back the recording and see if we got anything.'

They sat down on the carpet and Jimmy rewound the tape recorder. He pressed play and they listened carefully.

As the first and second questions went by, they found themselves listening to silence in response. There was just the slight hum of the tape recorder. No voice.

'It doesn't sound like we got any voice phenomenons from Walter,' said Becky.

'It's phenomena, actually,' said Jimmy.

'You've been studying this ghost-hunting stuff far too hard.'

They listened carefully to Becky's voice saying the

third question: *'We think that you're angry because of something to do with Coral-Anne Thistlewick. Is that correct?'*

'Hang on, did you hear that?' asked Jimmy after a few seconds.

'What?' Becky asked eagerly.

'It was a sort of rustle.'

He rewound the tape and played the question again. Jimmy was right, there was definitely a noise.

They played it a third time. It was very faint, but it sounded like a low voice saying, 'Cor … An.'

'Is that Walter's voice?' asked Jimmy.

'I think so,' said Becky, excitement running through her. 'I think he was trying to say "Coral-Anne". Let's listen to the next question.'

They did: *'And does it have something to do with Little Lord Thistlewick, as well?'*

Immediately there was a sound. 'Little…'

Then several second's silence, followed by '…Lord.'

'Why did you poison Little Lord Thistlewick's horse, Walter?' Becky's voice came from the recorder.

'Gri … Gib … ns … f … m … d.'

The voice was very broken up. They played it again.

'It sounds like "Grinlin Gibbons" to me, but what was that last word?' asked Jimmy.

'I think he's saying "Grinlin Gibbons found",' said Becky. 'Like he found out it was Walter who poisoned the horse. Anyway, keep playing.'

Jimmy pressed play on the tape recorder. 'This was when we started to get uncomfortable, wasn't it?'

Becky nodded. Two seconds later, they found out why.

The noise that came out of the tape machine was louder than before. It seemed to scream out one word.

'Grinlin! Grinlin! Grinlin! Grinlin!'

'What's he trying to tell us?' asked Jimmy.

'I don't know – that he is angry with Grinlin Gibbons for finding out the truth?' said Becky.

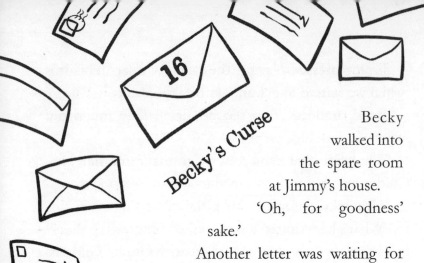

Becky walked into the spare room at Jimmy's house.

'Oh, for goodness' sake.'

Another letter was waiting for her on the floor.

The thought entered her mind: open it.

Open it? Should she risk it? She wanted to know what her curse would be – if the fishermen couldn't catch fish, if the carpenter couldn't cut wood, if her mum was losing the post office, then what would the curse be for Becky Evans, adventurer and ghost hunter?

'Open it. Go on.'

It was like a small voice inside her head getting louder.

No, she thought, *I can't.*

'Go on. It'll be fine.'

No.

'Open the letter!'

Before she knew it, Becky had her hand around the envelope, her finger in the fold. She tore it open.

Inside was a sheet of paper. A plain, white sheet. She turned it around, but there was no writing.

What would happen to her now?

She looked up from the paper and for a second didn't recognise where she was. All the furniture had been removed from the room, leaving only the empty, white walls and dark blue carpet.

'Who did that? Who's taken all the furniture? Mrs Cole?'

She turned around to open the door. But when she moved her hand to the doorknob, she saw with a shock that it wasn't there – the door had disappeared, replaced by a solid white wall.

Eyes wide, she walked back into the startling white room.

There was only one object – a painting, hanging on the wall. The one of Walter Anion from the loft. He glared down at her.

'Is this my curse, Walter?' she asked.

The white walls started to darken. They quickly changed into cold, rusty bars, as if Becky was in a cage or a prison cell.

She stared hard at the painting of Walter. It seemed to be coming towards her. But no, it wasn't just the painting – the bars of the cell were moving towards her too.

From somewhere outside she heard voices calling. 'Becky Evans.' 'It's all your fault.' 'You made him appear.'

'It's not my fault,' she tried to call back. 'He turned up because of Steve, not me.'

She turned around. On the opposite side was another

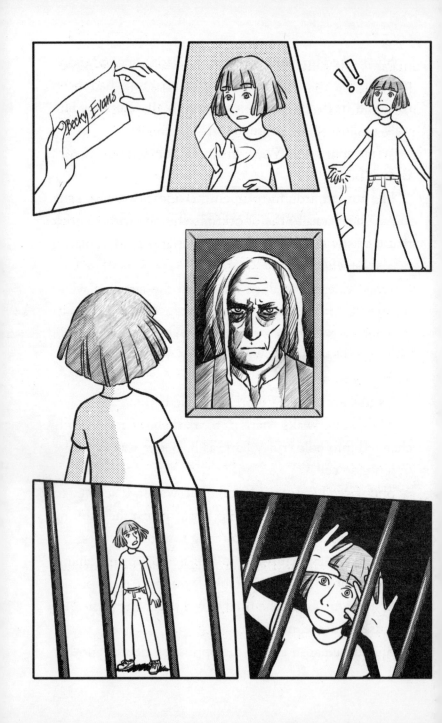

image – this time the one of Walter with Coral-Anne. The bars on that side were getting closer too. In fact, every time someone shouted from outside, the bars got nearer to her. She was going to be crushed!

'It's all your fault.' 'Becky Evans has cursed our island.' 'Becky! Becky!'

She ran towards the bars and threw herself against them. Solid metal. She fell backwards and landed in the centre of the rapidly decreasing cell.

'Why did I open the letter? Why?' she asked, half in anger, half in panic.

All four sides continued to move inwards as the voices got louder. She was blinded by fear. All she could see was a set of green eyes – Walter's eyes.

'Why are you doing this, Walter? Why are you cursing us?'

It was too much for her. Trying to escape the look in his eyes, she stared up to the ceiling. There wasn't one. Instead a huge brown envelope filled her vision. The big, spidery letters on it read:

Becky Evans

'Stop it, Walter, stop it!'

'Becky,' she heard the deep, angry voices call around her. 'Becky!'

Envelopes started flooding down towards her. Hundreds of them – brown ones, white ones, big, small – a storm of post.

She put her hands up to protect herself.

'Becky.'

The envelopes rose up, covering her whole body.

'Becky.'

She saw a final envelope fall towards her. It covered up her eyes, plunging her into darkness.

'Becky!'

'Stop it, Walter!'

'Becky, it's not Walter, it's Jimmy.'

Becky opened her eyes. She was lying down. Around her were the bed, the oak wardrobe and all the other things that were meant to be in the room. On the wall opposite her was the usual painting of the ship in a storm – not Walter's portrait. In front of her was a very concerned Jimmy.

'What ... what happened?' Becky asked, feeling feeble.

'I think you were having a nightmare,' said Jimmy. 'I heard you from my room. You were calling out.'

Becky sat up. 'So I didn't open the envelope?'

'No.'

'It was just a nightmare?'

'Yes,' replied Jimmy. 'What was it about?'

Becky told him, as clearly as she could.

'But was it a nightmare that my own mind created, or was it another of Walter's visions?' she finished.

'I think it was just you, Becky. You probably need to take it easy for a day or two.'

'No, there's no time for that. The voting for the destruction of the post office ends tomorrow,' said Becky. She felt wide awake now. 'I have to solve this curse, and I think I've got an idea.'

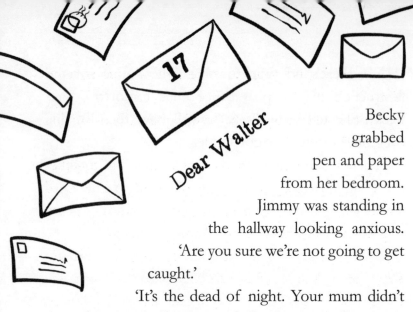

17

Dear Walter

Becky grabbed pen and paper from her bedroom. Jimmy was standing in the hallway looking anxious.

'Are you sure we're not going to get caught.'

'It's the dead of night. Your mum didn't hear us sneaking out of your house, and no one's going to come into the post office or the flat at this time.'

'So what's the plan?'

'We're going to write Walter a letter.'

'We tried that at the Calling,' said Jimmy.

'Well, in that letter I told him to stop his curse and go away,' said Becky. 'There were also thirty people there with us at the Calling, and he obviously didn't like them because he'd cursed them. I think it's similar to what happened in my nightmare earlier – I felt completely trapped in a cell, with loads of voices shouting in at me. That must be what it's like for Walter's ghost at the moment. First there was the Calling, then we tried to bottle him, and there's Mr Finch and all his ways of trying to trap Walter and make him go away. Maybe

Walter just wants someone to be nice – to understand him.'

'Why should we be nice to an evil ghost who is cursing everyone?'

'There's something that doesn't quite fit together about all this, and even if he did cause Little Lord Thistlewick's death, we need to find out why. I'm going to write him another letter – a more polite one.'

Under the light of a torch, she spent a few minutes constructing the letter in her neatest handwriting. She wrote that she wanted to hear Walter's side of the story. She asked him why he was angry, why he put the curse on the post office and what had happened when Little Lord Thistlewick's horse had been poisoned. She finished by writing, 'If there is anything that we can do to help you, please tell us.'

Becky took the letter to the spare room and left it lying on the rocking chair.

'Walter, I've written you a letter. A nice one,' she said, and walked out of the room.

The two children settled down in Becky's bedroom, because it was the one nearest to the spare room. If this was going to work, they would have to let Walter come to them.

Soon they grew tired. Becky let Jimmy use her bed, and she dragged in the mattress from the spare room and laid it out on the floor.

'You could have helped,' she said, collapsing onto the mattress.

'It was fun watching you struggle.' Jimmy grinned.

Becky got a torch and pen and paper ready, in case anything happened during the night that she needed to write down.

As they lay there trying to get to sleep, she started to wonder, *What if Walter Anion does turn up and he is angry with me again? What will he do this time?*

She decided not to tell Jimmy about her worries, but felt secure with him there beside her.

Soon he was snoring loudly, fast asleep. Becky sat and listened.

'If snoring could help get rid of the ghost, then you'd do a pretty good job,' she said to him, but he didn't hear.

After another fifteen minutes of snoring, Becky was getting pretty fed up.

'I need to get some sleep too,' she said.

She tried throwing a pillow at his head, but it didn't stop him.

Becky wasn't sure what time she drifted off to sleep, but it wasn't long before the familiar image of Coral-Anne Thistlewick appeared in front of her. It lasted for about thirty seconds, but then stopped, and her mind went blank again.

Is it you showing me that image, Walter? You need to show me more – I need to understand, she thought in her half-sleep.

130

Later that night, Becky opened her eyes. She wasn't sure if she was awake or still sleeping, but in front of her floated Walter Anion. He still looked just as terrifying, but somehow Becky knew he wasn't there to harm her. Glaring straight into her eyes, the ghost glided towards her. Becky felt her eyes closing.

As they did, she wasn't met with the darkness of the inside of her eyelids, but by the sight of a brilliant sunny day.

Walter's Story

'You want to know why I have cursed the post office. For once you have asked with seeming politeness, so I shall tell you.' It was Walter's voice, but it felt like it was coming from inside Becky's head.

Through the sunlight, the Thistlewick market square appeared. It looked different; the people were wearing old-fashioned clothes and there were fewer buildings – this was Thistlewick from Walter's time.

Outside the post office, a younger looking Walter stood. Becky almost didn't recognise him, because he seemed so happy. Around him an excited buzz passed through the market; the sellers stopped selling; the children stopped playing. Soon Becky saw why – a man strolled into the market, larger than life in his rich purple cloak. It was Lord Thistlewick himself. He walked over to Walter.

'Ladies and gentlemen,' his voice boomed. 'May I introduce you to the first postmaster of Thistlewick Island. Walter, I welcome you into my community with a warm heart and a friendly smile. May you prosper here.'

A cheer went up around the islanders. As Walter shook Lord Thistlewick's hand, a beautiful young woman caught his eye. It was Lady Coral-Anne Thistlewick, and she smiled kindly.

The image faded.

'I fell in love with her the first time I saw her smile, but it was almost four years before we grew close,' said Walter's ghostly voice.

Becky saw the market again. Walter and Coral-Anne were sitting on a bench at the centre, talking quietly.

'However kind and friendly Lord Thistlewick was, he could not approve of my relationship with his daughter. We were going against the grain of society, she a Lady, and me a lowly postmaster. The two of us did not care, though. We did not hide our affection. It was the most wonderful time of our lives and we had plans to marry.'

Becky saw another man walk into the edge of the market square. He had thick eyebrows and deep-set, glaring eyes.

'Lord Grinlin Gibbons,' Walter explained bitterly. 'A family friend of the Thistlewicks, who owned an estate on the mainland. He had his eyes set on Coral-Anne and thought that just because he was a Lord, she was his by rights. As my relationship with Coral-Anne grew deeper, Gibbons's trips here from the mainland became more frequent, and he asked her several times to marry him. Even though he was a Lord, in truth I suspected that Gibbons was not wealthy – he wanted to get his hands on the Thistlewick fortune, and would do anything to achieve this. It wasn't love, but greed, that made my Coral-Anne attractive to him, I was sure. Of course, she declined his offers – after all, she had just accepted my proposal of marriage. How wrong I was not to see Grinlin Gibbons as a real threat.'

The scene changed. The young Walter was walking around Thistlewick delivering post, accompanied by Coral-Anne Thistlewick. They talked joyfully about this and that, and at each house they went to, the residents came out to greet them.

'Although Lord Thistlewick refused to be a part of it, we continued our plans for our wedding and hoped to soon persuade him. Most of my friends on the island seemed happy for us, and my good friend, Solomon Starr, agreed to be my best man.'

As Walter and Coral-Anne walked along a coastal path a horse galloped up to them. Walter backed away slightly. Atop the horse, Becky recognised the young boy, Little Lord Thistlewick.

'One person I did not get along with was Little Lord Thistlewick,' said Walter. 'I tried my best, but I had a dislike of horses – I was bitten by one as a child – and the Little Lord was only friendly with those who shared his love of the creature. Knowing this, Gibbons decided to befriend the boy. On each of his trips over from the mainland, they went out riding together, and Gibbons helped to train the horses. That meant he was always there, threatening to spoil my happiness, grinning maliciously at me. Despite my position, I argued with him sometimes.'

Becky watched as the market appeared and the young Walter stormed across it towards Grinlin Gibbons.

'You leave Coral-Anne and me alone, Gibbons,' he shouted.

'Watch your tongue, Anion, and remember your position,' Gibbons replied coolly. 'She should be mine. You're just a postmaster. I am a Lord. I will have her one of these days.'

'I will not let you anywhere near her!'

Walter ran off, leaving Gibbons standing there, laughing deeply.

Next, Becky's mind was filled with an image of the post office. It looked quite different to how Becky was used to seeing it – there were no shelves with stationery or books. All of this was stored behind the large counter. Walter stood there writing in a logbook.

'It was five o'clock on Monday, August the second, 1717. I was just closing up the post office for the day, when ...'

Grinlin Gibbons entered the shop, a small brown parcel in his hand. Walter looked up.

'What are you doing here? Get out of my shop.'

'Whatever differences we have, Mr Anion, I am not here on personal matters,' Gibbons said smoothly. 'I have some business for you. This is a parcel for Little Lord Thistlewick. Sadly, I must leave now for a consultation on the mainland, so I would like you to deliver this to the Little Lord tomorrow. As you know, it is his birthday, and this is a surprise of sorts.'

Gibbons placed the parcel on the counter and threw down payment for it. His eyes flashed a dark expression at Walter.

'Good day,' he said, and left before the postmaster had a chance to respond.

Walter stared at the parcel.

'I was tempted to open it and find out what Gibbons was sending Little Lord Thistlewick,' said his ghost. 'But I could not. I had to follow post office regulations. I noticed that Gibbons had failed to write the address on the parcel. As it was against regulations to deliver a piece of post with no address, I took a pen and wrote it on myself. "Little Lord Thistlewick, Thistlewick House, Thistlewick Island". That was, it turned out, a foolish mistake – and a cunning ploy by Gibbons.

'The next day – Tuesday, August the third, 1717 – I delivered the parcel along with all the other birthday packages for Little Lord Thistlewick, and thought nothing more of it.'

Becky saw Walter back in his post office. The door opened and in came Coral-Anne in floods of tears. Walter walked over to her, deeply concerned.

'Whatever is the matter, my darling?'

'My brother … he … he's dead … fell off his horse.'

She collapsed into him and they hugged for many minutes.

'She was so sad,' said Walter's ghost. 'And I was sad with her. But how could I have known that this was to be the last time I would see my beautiful Coral-Anne? The next few days went by so quickly. The parcel I had delivered to Little Lord Thistlewick was found to contain poisoned horse feed. Not knowing this, the boy had given it to his horse, which collapsed later that day, throwing the boy off and killing him instantly. That poor child. Only then did I realise what Grinlin Gibbons's evil plan had been.

'It was my handwriting on the parcel, of course. I tried to explain what had happened, but on his return to the island Gibbons accused me of sending the poisoned feed myself. There was no evidence to prove otherwise – no one had seen him coming to the post office to hand it to me. Gibbons was a Lord, and I was just a postmaster, so he was believed. My relationship with Coral-Anne also went against me; Gibbons even had the audacity to say that I was after the Thistlewicks' money. I was arrested and quickly sentenced. Causing the death of a member of the Thistlewick family meant life imprisonment.'

Becky heard jeering and cheering, then saw Walter being led through the lanes of Thistlewick, handcuffed to a policeman. As they walked, people surrounded Walter, shouting, throwing rotten fruit at him. It was a horrible sight.

'You're evil!' … 'A sorcerer!' … 'You've cursed this island.'

'Gibbons turned them against me – the whole island,' Walter continued, his voice grave. 'If you put my initial and surname together, it makes wanion, which is an old English word meaning "curse". Because of that, they all thought I was an evil sorcerer who had put a curse on Little Lord Thistlewick. It hurt so much, all these people who had been my friends, now turned against me. What hurt me most was Solomon Starr.'

As Walter was walked through the market, a child ran out and threw a tomato at him. It dripped miserably down his coat.

'Sidney Evans, stop that at once,' a man said to the boy.

The boy, Becky realised, was one of her own ancestors.

The man who had told him off looked very much like the Mr Starr Becky knew, and was obviously Solomon.

Walter looked hopefully towards him, but Solomon didn't make eye contact. He turned his back on Walter.

'Solomon was my best friend, and even he believed Gibbons instead of me. I was led to the Thistlewick prison, my new home for the rest of my life. No one came to visit me – soon even the jeering and shouting from people outside my cell stopped. I had no friends left. I lived in hope of the truth being discovered – that it was Gibbons who had poisoned the horse, not me. Then, a year later, I was told that Coral-Anne – my dear Coral-Anne – was to be married to Gibbons. All my hope, my life as I had known it, had ended.

'I was only allowed one hobby. Painting had been my passion as a child so I chose that. I mostly painted horses – I do not know why – and these canvases were quickly removed from my cell. Over the years, I was occasionally able to find information about the outside world – from new prisoners and the kinder prison guards. I was told of Coral-Anne and Gibbons's first child, and their move away from Thistlewick. They didn't even return when Lord Thistlewick's death was announced. In my time, the father's estate was passed onto his firstborn son, but with Little Lord Thistlewick dead, the Thistlewick fortune went to Coral-Anne and Gibbons, which made him rich.

'My guards thought that my one hobby would be enough to keep me from going mad. They were wrong. Imagine it, seeing the same four walls day after day for years, without a friend in the world and knowing that the person you most love is married to the person you most despise. It is enough to send anyone mad. I became angry and bitter.

'It was after twenty-four years of imprisonment that I received my very first visitor.'

A Walter who had aged rapidly appeared in Becky's vision, standing in his tiny prison cell. He now had the angry look in his eyes that she recognised all too well. A man walked up to the bars of the cell, carrying with him a large case for a musical instrument, and peered in. Although he had greying hair and a number of wrinkles, Becky recognised the man as Solomon Starr.

'Walter,' Solomon whispered. 'My old friend, where do I begin, after all these years? I am sorry. The guards haven't given me long. I came to say that I believe you.'

Walter frowned at him.

'Yes, I believe you. I was foolish to listen to Lord Gibbons. I never fully believed him. I so wanted you to be innocent. And now, Walter, I have found evidence which not only proves your innocence, but also Lord Gibbons's guilt. I have tried to make this evidence known publicly, but Gibbons stopped me – he is in control of this island now, even though he never steps foot on it.

But Walter, I know that he set you up; he framed you for the murder of Little Lord Thistlewick.'

'One more minute,' the gruff voice of a prison guard came from the other end of the corridor.

A look of urgency spread across Solomon Starr's face. 'I have brought this for you.'

He opened his instrument case, and instead of a musical instrument, he pulled out an ornate painting frame and slipped it through the bars. Walter took it and slowly turned it around in his hands.

'Gibbons has wiped all trace of you from this island, Walter. Paint a portrait of yourself and put it in this frame.'

The sound of footsteps echoed down the corridor.

'It's the prison guard,' said Solomon. 'I must go.'

As he moved away, he looked back to Walter and smiled at him. 'You were framed, my friend, you were framed.'

'I wish I had said something to Solomon,' came the voice of Walter's ghost again. 'But I could not bring myself to. I was too far gone. I did as he suggested – I painted a portrait of myself from the reflection in my water bowl and put it in the frame Solomon had given me. When I looked at the portrait I saw how angry I was, and I thought only one thing: I did not know how, but I would take my revenge on Gibbons and all the people who turned against me. If they thought I was a wanion

– a curse – then I would curse them. Solomon Starr would be saved – I forgave him – but the rest would be cursed. I hid the painting under a floorboard in my cell, so that the guards would not take it away.

'Later that year, I died. My anger led me to leave a ghost behind. Gibbons was long gone, and I knew I did not have much strength in me, even as a ghost. I attached myself to my painting. Many years later, the painting was found where I had hidden it and taken to the post office. There I waited, until I was stirred into action by the descendant of Grinlin, Steven Gibbons. I found myself too late to curse those who turned against me, so I have done the next best thing – cursed their descendants, who seem just as horrible as they were. You were helpful in spreading my curse, of course, by delivering the letters last Wednesday morning.'

Becky felt a strange sensation as Walter left her mind. She opened her eyes and saw him floating in front of her.

'So now, Rebecca Evans, you know the truth about my curse.'

With that, Walter Anion's ghost disappeared into thin air.

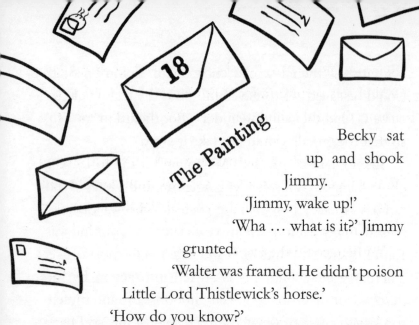

18
The Painting

Becky sat up and shook Jimmy.

'Jimmy, wake up!'

'Wha … what is it?' Jimmy grunted.

'Walter was framed. He didn't poison Little Lord Thistlewick's horse.'

'How do you know?'

'Walter has just shown me a vision of what really happened.'

Jimmy looked doubtful. 'You just imagined it, surely? Like your nightmare.'

'I think I know where we can find proof that Walter is innocent. Come with me.'

They threw on their clothes and went into the hallway. Becky lowered the ladder to the loft and they climbed up. She shone her torchlight over the painting of Walter Anion – the painting she now knew he had painted himself, in the frame given to him by Solomon Starr.

'Solomon said he had evidence proving it was Grinlin Gibbons who sent the poisoned horse feed and framed Walter,' Becky thought out loud. 'The exact words

Solomon used were "you were framed", then he gave Walter this picture frame. I don't think it is an ordinary frame, though. I think that Solomon hid his evidence in it, somehow.'

Becky picked up the painting and turned it around in her hands. The back was just a plain piece of wood. She tried pulling each of the sides of the frame, but they didn't move.

'Where could the evidence be hidden?'

Jimmy pointed to the bottom of the frame. 'What's that?'

Becky felt along the bottom and came to a raised bump. Closer inspection revealed it was a catch. She dug her fingernail into it and prised the catch open. The bottom of the frame creaked outwards. Out of the gap it left, a piece of rolled-up paper fell.

'Look,' said Becky. 'There's writing on the paper. It's evidence!'

'What does it say?' asked Jimmy.

The top line read:

Records of The Crystal Apothecary, Blackbeach Island. Owner: Anthony Crystal

Under this was a list of orders placed at the Apothecary in the month of August, 1717. The writing was faded and hard to read. Becky put her finger next to the list of customer names and slowly moved down it. She missed the name she was looking for at first, but then found it close to the top of the page:

Date: Monday 2nd August 1717 ... Customer: Lord G. Gibbons ... Product: 2 Litres Arsenic for rat infestation

'Remember what Mr Morris said when he was trying to catch rats at the island hall? Arsenic was used as rat poison in the olden times,' said Becky.

Jimmy nodded. 'He said it was also poisonous to other animals.'

'And do you recognise that date, Jimmy – the second of August?' Becky asked, excited.

'It's the day before Little Lord Thistlewick died.'

'So Grinlin Gibbons bought the poison, which he mixed with the horse feed in the parcel he gave to Walter to deliver. Walter was telling the truth – he's innocent. It makes sense now. Walter is angry because of what Grinlin Gibbons did, and how all his friends rejected him.'

'That's why he's put the curse on the people he has, isn't it?' said Jimmy.

'Yes, he's cursed the descendants of the people who turned their back on him when he was alive. But why wasn't Steve cursed?' asked Becky. 'He is Grinlin Gibbons's descendant.'

'He's also Coral-Anne Thistlewick's descendant,' Jimmy pointed out. 'On the one hand, Walter's ghost would want to take revenge on Steve for being related to Lord Gibbons, but on the other hand, Walter would never harm someone related to Coral-Anne Thistlewick.'

'And he didn't curse Mr Starr's parcel, because his ancestor, Solomon Starr, is the only person who believed Walter was innocent. Walter might even have sent the medicine to Mr Starr to say thank you.'

'It doesn't sound like he wants to stop cursing the other people, though, does it?' said Jimmy.

'No. But there has to be a way to get him to stop.'

'Can you smell smoke?' asked Jimmy.

'What?'

'I can smell smoke.'

Becky sniffed the air, and she too could sense something burning. 'Maybe someone's having a bonfire.'

'In the middle of the night?' Jimmy frowned. 'I … I think it's coming from downstairs.'

They looked at each other, and the same thought flashed through their minds. They both clambered out of the loft as fast as they could. The smell intensified as they went and Becky could hear a faint crackling noise.

'I don't think it's coming from the flat,' said Jimmy

'It's coming from the post office!' Becky shouted.

She fumbled with the lock on the door that led from the flat to the shop.

'Is it Walter?' Jimmy shouted to her. 'Is he angry with us?'

'I don't know.'

The lock clicked open. Becky burst through the door.

'Becky.' Jimmy caught up with her and handed her a blanket. 'Take this and wrap it round yourself. It'll protect you against flames. Be careful!'

They crept down the stairs. The crackling sounded like enormous fingers crumpling newspaper.

The main post office was as it should be – the rows of stationery and packaging untouched. But coming from the sorting room behind the counter was a strong red glow.

'Walter, stop!' Becky called.

She ran towards the sorting room but froze in the entrance as a wall of heat hit her. She shielded her eyes and squinted in horror at the sight in front of her. All the shelves and boxes, all the spare envelopes and parcels kept in the room, were on fire. Flames lashed furiously up like fighting snakes.

Becky knew she had to do something fast, but she was too stunned.

'I'll … I'll get some water,' said Jimmy. 'We need to stop the fire spreading.'

He leapt out through the post office door. Becky continued to stare at the mass of red.

Then she saw something else. Through the flames, at the other end of the sorting room, was a person. The flames were too bright to see who it was properly.

'Walter, is that you?'

Becky squinted – no, the figure was too small to be Walter. It was hunched over. Becky could just make out the features of a boy's face.

'Finn?'

'I … I had to do something,' the boy said, barely audible over the sound of the fire. 'Your curse is preventing my granddad from fishing, Walter Anion. If he can't fish, he'll lose his job. I have to stop you.'

It *was* Finn.

'No, Finn, you can't! It'll just make him angrier,' she called.

Finn looked up.

'Becky, is that you?' he cried. 'I'm sorry. I didn't know anyone else was here. I'm sorry … I couldn't think what else to do.'

He seemed to collapse against the wall as he spoke.

Becky looked around the room. Seriously panicking, she realised that Finn was trapped behind the flames. He couldn't escape.

They had to get him out.

'Stay there.'

She ran outside to where Jimmy was unravelling a hosepipe from the water supply in the market square. She turned on the water tap and helped him carry the pipe in through the post office. Water sprayed out everywhere.

With all their energy, they aimed the pipe at the sorting room fire.

***

'I'm sorry … I'm really sorry,' Finn kept saying.

'It's OK, Finn, you just need to rest now,' said Mayor Merryweather. 'I'll fetch Albert for you in a bit.'

'No, please don't tell Granddad. He'll be so ashamed of me,' said Finn. 'I couldn't think of what else to do. Nothing else we tried worked. I thought this was the only way to stop Walter Anion and his curse.'

'I understand,' said Becky. She knew exactly what it was like to be so frustrated with Walter Anion.

'I'm sorry I was so mean to you,' said Finn. 'I know it wasn't your fault that the ghost turned up.'

'Don't worry, we'll find a way to stop the curse soon,' she replied.

Mr Morris walked out of the sorting room, from where damp smoke was still curling out.

'Looks like it's all clear in there,' he said. 'I've dampened everything down again, but you did an amazing job, children. If you hadn't found the fire when you did, it would have spread over the whole building, and Finn … well … I dread to think what would have happened.'

Finn lowered his head and sat in silence.

'You were both really brave,' said the mayor. 'I'm proud of you.'

'Anyone would have done what we did,' said Jimmy.

Becky turned to her friend and hugged him. 'I don't

think I could have done it without you, Jimmy. Thank you.'

They sat quietly, huddled in blankets, and Becky thought about Walter and his tragic story. He had been wrongly accused of killing someone. Then he had lost the woman he loved and everyone on Thistlewick – all his friends – had turned against him. It was heartbreaking. Becky would never have been able to cope being so lonely, without Mum or Jimmy or any of her other friends. No wonder Walter was so angry.

'That's it!' she exclaimed. 'It's simple.'

'What is, Becky?' asked Jimmy.

'I was right – Walter needs us to be nice to him. All this time, since he was accused of poisoning Little Lord Thistlewick's horse, he's been rejected.' She turned to the mayor. 'Mayor Merryweather, I think I've got a plan.'

She told him and Jimmy what she was thinking.

The mayor nodded. 'That sounds like an excellent idea. I will gather everyone we need.'

'But there's someone else we'll need too,' said Becky. 'I have to go and get Steve.'

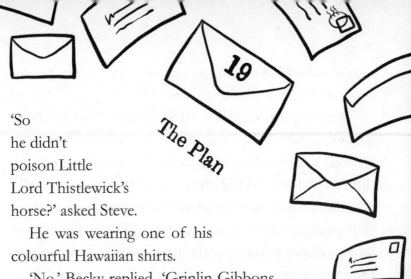

'So he didn't poison Little Lord Thistlewick's horse?' asked Steve.

He was wearing one of his colourful Hawaiian shirts.

'No,' Becky replied. 'Grinlin Gibbons set Walter up.'

Steve frowned. 'How do you know he wasn't lying? He's probably trying to make you feel sorry for him so he can carry on his curse. I wouldn't put it past Walter Anion.'

She showed Steve the piece of paper – Solomon's evidence.

'It was only when he was imprisoned for the crime that Grinlin Gibbons committed that he became angry,' she explained.

'Blimey,' Steve puffed out his cheeks. 'All this time I thought Walter Anion was evil, and now I find out it was actually Grinlin Gibbons. My ancestor. That's quite hard to take in. But I suppose it happened a long time ago. It's all in the past.'

'Except it isn't, is it?' said Becky. 'It's the reason Walter's back now.'

151

'Yes, that's true.'

'And I have a plan to stop the curse.'

Steve leaned forwards. 'You've figured out a way to get rid of him?'

'No, that was the problem – we've been trying to get him to go away. But people only leave ghosts behind if they have unfinished business, or if they're particularly unhappy, don't they? I think what Walter really needs is for people to find out the truth, and to apologise for rejecting him.'

'But that's not possible. All the people who supposedly rejected him will be long dead.'

'Their descendants are still alive, though – they are who Walter has been cursing. We need them to tell Walter they're sorry for what their ancestors did. And that includes you, Steve.'

'Why me?' he moaned.

'Because you are Grinlin Gibbons's descendant. You have to apologise for him.'

'I told you, I can't go back to the post office, even if what you say is true. Walter will still try to harm me,' said Steve.

'No he won't. Don't forget that you're Coral-Anne's descendant as well as Grinlin's. As long as you say you're sorry, like everyone else, it will be fine.'

Steve stared at Becky for a long time.

'OK,' he said finally. 'You've got this far and you've

done incredibly well. So I trust what you're saying. And I suppose I am sorry for him. What do I have to do?'

Becky explained that everyone was writing letters to Walter, telling him that they understood what had actually happened and were sorry that their ancestors treated him so badly.

She took out pen and paper and watched as Steve wrote his letter. With a little help from her, he got it finished quickly:

Dear Walter,

My name is Steven Gibbons. I am a descendant of Coral-Anne and Grinlin Gibbons. Until today, I did not know the truth about how Grinlin framed you and accused you of poisoning Little Lord Thistlewick. It is horrible and I am truly sorry he did this, and that I thought you were guilty.

I only hope you accept my apology.

Yours,

Steven Gibbons

***

When Becky arrived back at the flat with Steve, there was a long queue of people waiting in the hallway. Albert was at the centre of the queue with Finn, who looked calmer now. Mr Finch was standing behind them biting his lip. Becky had figured out how to solve the curse just in time – when she had last looked at his 'destruction' plan on the post office door, there were more names in the 'for' column than in the 'against', and the voting was to have ended that afternoon.

Jimmy walked over to her. 'Everyone's ready. They have all written letters, like you said.'

'Great, shall we start?' She looked to Steve.

'I'll wait here at the back,' he said, fidgeting nervously. 'But Becky, you might want to use this.'

Steve gave her a small video camera.

'Jimmy will be better with this than me.' She passed the camera to him.

'Do you want me to film it all?' asked Jimmy.

'Yes, but that's not just any old camera,' said Steve. 'It's a thermal-imaging camera. It shows you the temperature of everything it films. Most objects don't have much energy in them…'

'So they come out green and blue, don't they?' asked Jimmy.

'That's right,' said Steve. 'How did you know?'

'He knows all about ghost hunting now, he's been reading up on it,' said Becky.

Steve grinned at him and almost looked proud. 'So I suppose you know that objects with a bit more energy appear yellow in the camera?'

'And things with lots of energy look red, or if they

have even more energy, like people, the camera shows them as white,' Jimmy added.

'So we can use this to see if Walter turns up?' asked Becky.

'Yes,' Steve replied. 'You need to keep an eye on it and make sure he isn't lurking around waiting to attack people. If he's there, his energy will show up on the camera as a yellow or red mass.'

'I don't think he's going to attack anyone now they're trying to be kind to him,' said Becky.

Steve shook his head. 'Even so, I still don't trust him. A ghost that has created a curse like his is capable of anything. He still could get angry.'

'So what do we do if he does get angry, or threatens more curses?' asked Becky.

'If there's even the smallest hint that he's angry, you need to get out of the room as quickly as possible,' Steve said, a serious look on his face.

Becky watched Jimmy film around the hallway. He rewound the tape and showed her what he had filmed. Down the staircase everything from the banister to the post office shop beyond showed up as different shades of green and blue. But when the camera focussed on all the people in the hallway, they showed up as bright red and white shapes.

'Are you sure you're happy to do this with me?' Becky asked Jimmy.

'Yep,' he said, as confidently as possible.

They walked along the queue of islanders. Mr Potts tapped Becky on the shoulder.

'It's terrible what our ancestors did to Walter Anion, isn't it?' he said in a soft voice. 'I think we are doing the right thing.'

Becky nodded and moved to the front of the queue. As she went she felt all the nervous faces staring at her expectantly. It was all up to her and Jimmy now.

She turned around to face everyone.

'Right, let's start,' she said loudly. 'One at a time, you need to take your letter into the spare room and deliver it to Walter by placing it on the bed. Then you must walk straight out of the room.'

'Do we have to go in there? Can't you just take all our letters in together?' asked Mr Finch.

'No,' said Becky. 'It's important that Walter knows it was you who wrote the letters. If I took them all in I might think that I just made them up. But Jimmy and me will be in there making sure that his ghost doesn't harm anyone. Is everybody ready?'

She had hoped they would all cheer, but the atmosphere was too tense for that. She looked to Finn – he nodded at her.

All these people have been affected by the curse, she reminded herself. *They need this plan to work. So do I, if I stand any chance of saving the post office.*

No pressure, then.

Becky pushed open the door and she and Jimmy walked into the spare room.

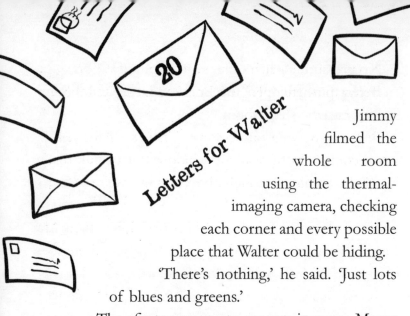

20

Letters for Walter

Jimmy filmed the whole room using the thermal-imaging camera, checking each corner and every possible place that Walter could be hiding.

'There's nothing,' he said. 'Just lots of blues and greens.'

The first person to come in was Mayor Merryweather. He carried a legal-looking letter.

'This document declares that you, Walter, are innocent. It states that you were wrongly convicted of killing Little Lord Thistlewick. The Thistlewick Island records have also been updated to show your innocence,' the mayor said to the room. 'We are all truly sorry.'

Mr Morris followed and placed her single sheet of paper carefully down. He moved out and Mr Starr came in.

'You didn't have to come, Mr Starr,' said Becky. 'Walter forgave your ancestor.'

'I would like to give Walter this,' Mr Starr replied, holding a small painting. 'Solomon kept it safe.'

As he put it on the bed, Becky saw that the painting was of the young Walter and Solomon Starr. They had their arms around each other and were both beaming.

'Everything still OK?' Becky asked Jimmy as Mr Starr left the room.

'It's still showing safe colours. There's a faint yellow beam coming from near the window, but I think that's just light coming through the curtains. We're safe to carry on.'

Mr Potts came in, then Albert and Finn, then Mr Finch. Five more people delivered letters, and there was still no sign of Walter. Although Becky knew this was a good thing, because it meant they were safe, she was getting concerned that he wouldn't show up at all. There was always the possibility that he might ignore all the letters and carry on his curse.

But then Becky thought back to his vision – how upset he had been when all those people had turned against him. She was sure that all he wanted was for everyone to apologise.

Steve entered the room, shuffling nervously along the floor towards the bed.

'Any sign of him?' he asked.

Jimmy shook his head.

'It's safe,' said Becky.

Steve placed his letter on the bed on top of the growing collection.

'I'm the final person from outside, Becky, so you're the only one left who needs to put their letter down.'

He walked quickly towards the door.

'Steve, I'm worried that Walter's not going to turn up at all. Can you sense him?'

Steve turned around and faced the room. His eyes focussed on different areas, his brow furrowed in concentration.

'I can sense something,' he said. 'I think he does know what we're doing.'

Steve walked out, the door closing behind him. Becky and Jimmy were on their own.

'Right, Walter. Everyone else has given you their letters. Mine is the final one.'

Becky placed it on the bed and read through what she had written one final time.

Dear Walter,

Thank you for showing me your vision. I understand now why you are so angry.

I have brought everyone together who has been affected by your curse. They are all sorry for what their ancestors did to you, and I am truly sorry that Sidney Evans threw rotten fruit at you. I hope our letters will make you feel happier.

Becky

She moved towards the door and looked back to the room.

'Come on, Jimmy, let's go.'

'I'll just do one last scan with the camera,' he replied.

As he focussed the camera on the window, he froze.

'Becky, that yellow light from the window has turned orange. It's getting bigger.'

Steve's warning flashed through her mind: *If there's even the smallest hint that he's angry, you need to get out of the room as quickly as possible.*

'I think it's time for us to leave.'

Becky put her hand on the doorknob and turned it. But it wouldn't turn. It was locked shut.

Her heart turned to ice as she remembered when this had last happened – *when Walter appeared the first time.*

'Walter? Is that you?'

She looked around the room and couldn't see anything unusual.

'Becky,' said Jimmy. 'The orange light has turned red. It's starting to move away from the window.'

'Show me,' she said, and ran over to him.

He pulled out the camera screen and they both watched the red mass creeping towards them.

They moved back as far as they could, pressing themselves against the door.

The red mass was starting to take more of a human shape in the camera image now. It moved slowly towards the bed. Becky stared at the letters. They started to twitch.

'Is he reading them?' asked Jimmy.

'I hope so,' said Becky.

A large gust of wind swept through the room and made the camera shake in Jimmy's hand. It hadn't come through the window, because that was firmly shut.

'This can't be good,' Becky grabbed hold of Jimmy. 'He's angry, isn't he?'

The room suddenly became cold. Shivering, Becky realised what was happening.

'Walter is sucking up all the energy from the room. He's going to attack me.'

'Then he'll have to get past me, first!' said Jimmy, with more confidence than Becky had ever seen in him before.

She looked through the camera again. Walter's red shape, leaning over the bed, was expanding. Then the camera screen went blank – the camera had turned off. Jimmy hurriedly tried to turn it on again, but he couldn't.

'Walter's sucked all the life out of the camera battery too!'

Becky looked to the bed again. The top letter – Becky's letter – rose slowly in the air and started to vibrate. *Just like at the Calling.* It was joined by a second letter, then another, and they swept through the air. Soon all the pieces of paper were spinning round.

They started to pick up speed.

'I'm not feeling good,' said Jimmy, all power draining from his voice.

Becky suddenly felt weak too – very weak, like she hadn't eaten for days. Walter was even using their energy now.

They collapsed to the ground.

The wind that swept around the room was becoming unbearable. Becky found it hard to keep her eyes open. She didn't know what Walter was going to do. The two children clung together and closed their eyes tightly.

'I'm sorry, Walter,' Becky called out, but she could barely hear herself over the wind.

She braced herself.

'If you're going to curse me, just do it quickly,' she shouted.

Then, the wind stopped.

For a few seconds, Becky kept her eyes shut.

When she opened them she saw the room as if it was frozen. The letters were hanging in mid-air, all opened out.

But there was something else at the centre of them. Becky squinted to see. It was a pair of eyes.

What happened next may only have lasted for a second – even less than that – but she saw it clearly.

Walter's face was there, his green eyes staring at her. But they weren't angry or full of hatred now. They seemed peaceful – not quite happy, but somehow accepting. His face reminded Becky of the young Walter she'd seen in the painting with Coral-Anne, and the one with Solomon.

The ghost nodded at her and she understood – he was satisfied with the letters, and now it was his time to move on.

Another gust of air blew through the room and the letters all floated down to the floor, as Walter Anion faded away.

For a while there was silence; Becky just sat there.

She turned to Jimmy. 'You can open your eyes now. He's gone. It worked!'

Slowly, Jimmy blinked and looked around the room.

There was a thunder of banging on the door.

'Becky, what's going on?' called Steve. 'Can you open the door?'

She stood up and turned the doorknob. The door swung smoothly open. A dozen concerned faces were staring at her.

'Are you OK?' Steve asked.

'We're fine.' She grinned. 'Everything's fine.'

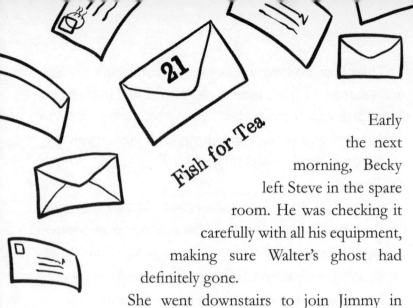

21

Fish for Tea

Early the next morning, Becky left Steve in the spare room. He was checking it carefully with all his equipment, making sure Walter's ghost had definitely gone.

She went downstairs to join Jimmy in the post office. He was sweeping up the charred remains of the sorting room fire.

Becky would have a lot of explaining to do when Mum got home – that was if this was still their home and Mum was still the postmistress, of course. It all depended on whether Walter's curse was still affecting things.

Although Becky was confident that his ghost was now gone for good, she still wasn't sure about the curse. There had been no signs yet that it had ended.

'Becky, look at this,' said Jimmy.

Out of the bits of blackened wood and cardboard on the floor, he pulled out a brand-new envelope – it hadn't been touched by fire at all.

'That's odd,' said Becky. 'How come that looks so new?'

'It's addressed to you.' Jimmy handed it to her.

She stared at the familiar, spidery writing that spelled out her name. 'I guess there's one way we can find out whether the curse has ended or not. I'll open this letter.'

'Are you sure?' asked Jimmy.

'Positive.'

Before she had time to change her mind, Becky took a deep breath and ripped the envelope open. Out of it, she pulled a white sheet of paper. It was blank apart from two small words:

Thank you.

The sound of footsteps came down the stairs and Steve appeared in the post office.

'There's no sign of him up there,' he said. 'I think he's gone.'

'I know he has,' said Becky. 'And he's at peace.'

They all spent the next half an hour in the sorting room, gradually cleaning it up and chatting merrily.

Becky stopped talking when she heard the post office door open. She looked up.

'Mum!'

Becky ran over and wrapped her arms around her tightly.

'Is the post office safe, Mum?' asked Becky.

'Yes, love. It was confirmed this morning, we can carry on running it,' said Mum, beaming.

Becky breathed a huge sigh of relief.

'But what on earth has been going on here?' asked Mum. 'I've just seen the notice outside calling for the post office to be knocked down. And my goodness, look at my sorting room!' Then she saw Steve. 'What is he doing here?'

He smiled guiltily at her.

'Don't be angry, Mum. It's a long story,' said Becky.

'A very long story,' said Jimmy.

As soon as they moved away from the door, it swung quickly open again and in burst Albert. He was wearing his fishing gear and his hair was windswept.

He started dancing around the shelves, knocking pencils and rubbers flying.

Finn walked in behind him. He went straight over to Becky and gave her a huge, fishy-smelling hug.

'Thank you!' Finn said.

'That's, er … OK,' said Becky, slightly taken aback.

'Albert, what are you …?' Mum began.

A smile stretched across old Albert's face. 'Look what I caught! Look what I caught!'

He skipped over to Becky and held out a large, lifeless fish.

'Well … we know what we're having for tea, then,' said Mum, bemused.

Becky started giggling. Then Jimmy joined in, and soon none of them could stop themselves laughing.

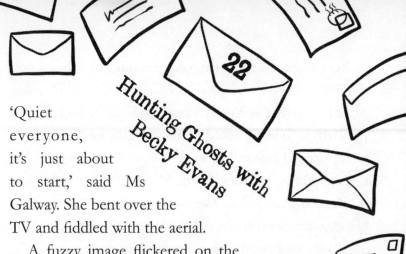

'Quiet everyone, it's just about to start,' said Ms Galway. She bent over the TV and fiddled with the aerial.

A fuzzy image flickered on the screen and an excited murmur stretched back through the large crowd at the White Wing. The pub was packed. Most of the island had turned up to see the show.

Sitting at the front, Becky grinned at Jimmy and reflected back on everything that had happened. When Becky's mum had arrived back from the mainland, they had told her the whole story, with help from Steve. Becky suspected that Mum didn't quite believe *everything* they said, but two hours later Mum had taken Steve to one side to have a private chat.

When they came back they were both grinning.

'Becky, I know how much you would love to be on TV,' Mum had said, 'so Steve has something to tell you.'

'Yes, I do,' Steve had said. 'I would like you, and Jimmy, to be the presenters for the Thistlewick Island episode of *Hunting Ghosts*.'

'I'd prefer not to,' Jimmy replied quickly. 'But could I film it?'

'Of course. But Becky, what about you?' asked Steve.

She had been speechless for several moments, then she'd hugged him.

Now she was sitting in the White Wing, watching as the title sequence for *Hunting Ghosts with Spooky Steve* played, and her own face appeared on the screen.

'Look, it's Becky!' Albert exclaimed.

Another wave of excitement went around the pub.

'We're here on Thistlewick Island, and we haven't just been having an amazing time, it's been the most incredible experience of my life!' said Steve, standing next to Becky on the TV. 'This episode is going to be unique, because for the first time ever I won't be presenting it. Let me introduce you to Becky Evans. She is a remarkable young lady and she will be your presenter. So, welcome to *Hunting Ghosts with Becky Evans*!'

The camera zoomed in to focus on Becky.

'I live on Thistlewick Island. I've always been told it was one of the most haunted places in the world, but I didn't believe that until recently…'

Once she'd got over how bizarre it was to see herself on TV, Becky was impressed with her presenting skills.

As the episode continued, she took the crew, with Jimmy filming, on a tour of Thistlewick, pointing out some of the parts that were said to be haunted. Then she conducted an interview with Albert about the ghosts he'd seen out at sea, and went out on a fishing trip with him. A huge grin appeared on his face every time he caught another fish.

Mayor Merryweather told Becky about lots of other ghosts that haunted the island and there was, of course, the footage of Steve's ghost hunt to find Little Lord Thistlewick.

Craig, the director, feeling unusually guilty about the way he had treated Becky, even let her choose the music for the episode. She had decided to use pieces performed entirely by Mr Starr on his violin. Watching it on TV now, she saw his face fill with pride.

The main focus of the episode was Becky and Jimmy's story about Walter Anion. Becky thought that after so many years of feeling rejected, he would have been honoured to have his true story told.

Although Jimmy hadn't wanted to present the show with her, he did agree to be interviewed.

He and Becky told Walter's story as accurately as they could. The episode ended by showing the footage of Walter that Jimmy had filmed using the thermal-imaging camera – it was the best filmed example of a ghost that Steve had ever seen.

'And that brings us to the end of *Hunting Ghosts* with me, Becky Evans,' Becky said at the end of the episode. 'Hasn't it been *amazing*?!'

Everyone at the White Wing clapped loudly as the credits rolled.

'Three cheers for Becky,' shouted Mr Potts.

Becky was lifted up onto a table and the cheer that erupted around the room deafened her.

She grinned down at Jimmy and saw her Mum next to him looking very proud.

***

'Do you still want to be a TV star, Becky?' Jimmy asked as they walked back from the pub that evening. 'I think you'd be brilliant at it!'

'No, I don't think so,' Becky replied. 'I only wanted to be a TV presenter so that I could travel around and have adventures. But now I don't need to do that, because there are loads of adventures waiting for me right here on Thistlewick.'

'Well, if you ever decide to go hunting for another ghost, let me know,' said Jimmy.

'I will,' said Becky.

'Not that I actually want to see another ghost. But someone has to keep you safe.' Jimmy grinned.

'Oh, I've just remembered, there's something I need to do. I'll see you in a bit.'

Becky ran along the coastal path and up Watersplash Lane to the island hall just in time to see Mayor

Merryweather standing by the entrance.

'Hello, Becky. Congratulations on the TV show, you were fantastic,' he said.

'Thank you. Do you still have that ghost-hunting book?' she asked.

'Eric's old notebook, you mean? I certainly do – would you like it?'

'Yes, please.'

The mayor popped into his office and came back with the small black book. 'I'm sure Eric would be honoured for me to give it to you – Thistlewick's new ghost hunter.'

When Becky got home, she attached a label to the cover of the notebook, which read: *Becky Evans: Ghost Hunter.*

She spent the whole evening looking through the notebook. At the back she found a page titled 'Ghosts Seen On Thistlewick'. There were a lot of names in a list, some with ticks next to them. At the bottom of the list she wrote the name 'Walter Anion' and put a tick next to it.

Becky slowly read through the rest of the names – there must have been at least a hundred. A grin spread accross her face as she thought of the adventures she was now going to have finding all those other ghosts.

Meet The 'Real' Spooky Steve!

To discover more about Steve, go to:

www.spookysteve.co.uk

Luke Temple with Steve

Turn over to read the first chapter
of Becky's next adventure...

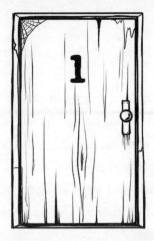

People Are Coming

'There are people coming!' Thatch shouted, floating into the third floor bedroom as fast as he could manage.

'People!' Peter shrieked.

'Careful, Peter. Don't use up too much energy,' said Willow, placing her hand on his shoulder to calm him.

'Will we have new friends to play with?' Rose asked eagerly. 'Is one of the people a girl?'

'It's a girl and a boy,' said Thatch.

'How old are they? Are they my age?' asked Peter, now bouncing up and down.

'The girl looks about Rose's age, the boy about my age.' Thatch grinned.

Rose span around in excitement. Peter stopped bouncing and his eyes welled up. No one his age ever came; he was always left out.

'Don't be such a cry baby,' said Thatch.

'Be kind to Peter,' Willow said sternly. 'He's only young.'

Peter had been six years old when he died. Willow still remembered watching it happen, seeing him panic, unable to help – she had never cried so much. That must have been over forty years ago.

Thatch rolled his eyes. 'We're all ghosts, what difference does age make? I've been stuck here much longer than he has.'

Willow looked down at the floor. Suddenly, any excitement about the people coming towards the house disappeared, replaced with a great fear. She had been in the house longer than all the other ghosts – over ninety years. She knew all too well what happened to people who stepped through the front door.

'Are they definitely coming this way?' Willow whispered.

'I saw them out the front.' Thatch hovered eagerly by the door. 'Come on, we need to get moving, or we'll never reach the front door in time to see them come in.'

'Is it safe to move?' asked Willow. '*He* isn't about, is *he*?'

'No, I think *he* is sleeping. We're safe.'

Thatch, Willow, Rose and Peter moved out of the room.

The procession down the stairs was slow. The ghosts needed energy to move; they mainly got this from the heat around them, but there wasn't much of that about at the moment. The house was almost unbearably dark and cold.

Only Thatch had found a way to conserve energy whilst moving quickly.

When they reached the second floor landing, Willow held onto Rose and Peter's hands. She never felt safe wandering around the house, and always stayed alert to danger. Thatch sailed through the air ahead of them. Willow knew he enjoyed the risk of moving from room to room.

'Slow down,' she said through gritted teeth. '*He* will notice us.'

'If you want to miss seeing these people arrive, fine,' Thatch replied in his loudest voice. 'Anyway, stop fretting – I haven't seen *him* for ages.'

'I have felt *his* presence around us,' said Willow. Rose nodded. 'And if new people are coming, you know *he* will be desperate to get to them before we do.'

Thatch glared at her and soared down the next flight of stairs.

Willow looked around cautiously. Gripping the two younger ghosts tightly, she calculated the best place to hide if *he* appeared, before travelling towards the front door. Thatch was there, gazing out of a small pane of glass.

'Can you see them?' asked Peter nervously.

'Do they seem playful?' asked Rose.

'Quiet, you two, I'm trying to look,' said Thatch.

The other ghosts glided up to the window and peered out together.

Thatch was right – a boy and a girl. It was too dark to see them properly, but Willow squinted her eyes and stared closely. The boy was tall and thin, with short blonde hair that was almost spiky. Willow didn't know much about boys, but this one had a look on his face that reminded her of Thatch in a bad mood. The girl had a mop of hazelnut hair, pushed back from her face, revealing shining eyes that Willow could only describe as adventurous.

'She's wearing trousers!' Rose exclaimed. 'Why is the girl dressed in boy's clothes?'

'Maybe girls do that now,' said Thatch.

Just then, the girl looked towards the house. All the ghosts gasped. Peter backed away. The girl was staring through the glass, directly at them.

'Can ... can she see us?' Peter asked breathlessly.

Thatch frowned. 'No, she ... she can't ... We don't have enough energy to be seen. Not even I do. We're too weak.'

The girl looked back at the boy, standing a few feet behind her.

'I thought not,' Thatch said more confidently. 'She was just staring at the house, not us.'

'Listen. The boy is speaking,' said Rose, pressing her ear to the glass.

'You've got to be joking, Becky,' they heard him say.

The girl grinned at him. 'Come on! You're the one who said we should come this way, Finn.'

Becky and Finn, Willow thought, fear now running through her. *Please do not come any closer. Run away! Do not enter this house!*

But Becky and Finn do enter Thicket House!
To discover what happens to them, you'll have to read

DOORWAY TO DANGER

To find out more about Luke Temple and his books, visit his website:

www.luketemple.co.uk

Do you want to discuss Ghost Post?
Here are some questions that might help!

1. Why do you think Becky is the main character in the book, rather than Jimmy or Finn?

2. Would you like to live on Thistlewick Island? Why?

3. Spooky Steve is an experienced ghost hunter. Why do you think he is so scared of Walter Anion's ghost?

4. How would you feel if you were cursed by Walter?

5. By the end of the book, had your opinion of Walter changed? If so, how?

6. Eric's ghost-hunting notebook contains a list of 'Ghosts Seen On Thistlewick'. What else do you think might be in the notebook?

7. How is *Ghost Post* similar or different to other ghost stories you have read?

8. What do you think will happen in Becky's next adventure?